If offer card is missing, write to: Silhouette Reader Service, 3010 Walden Ave, PO Box 1867, Buffalo, NY 14240-1867

THE SILHOUETTE READER SERVICE™ - HERE'S HOW IT WORKS:

Accepting free books places you under no obligation to buy anything. You may keep the books and gift and return the shipping statement marked "cancel". If you do not cancel, about a month later we'll send you 6 additional novels, and bill you just $2.67 each plus 25¢ delivery per book and applicable sales tax, if any.* That's the complete price–and compared to cover prices of $3.25 each–quite a bargain! You may cancel at any time, but if you choose to continue, every month we'll send you 6 more books, which you may either purchase at the discount price…or return to us and cancel your subscription.

*Terms and prices subject to change without notice. Sales tax applicable in N.Y.

You'll love this exquisite necklace, set with an elegant simulated pearl pendant! It's the perfect accessory to dress up any outfit, casual or formal — and is yours ABSOLUTELY FREE when you accept our NO-RISK offer!

PLAY "LUCKY 7"

**Just scratch off the silver box with a coin.
Then check below to see the gifts you get.**

YES! I have scratched off the silver box. Please send me all the gifts for which I qualify. I understand I am under no obligation to purchase any books, as explained on the back and on the opposite page.

215 CIS CA94
(U-SIL-R-09/97)

NAME

ADDRESS   APT.

CITY   STATE   ZIP

7	7	7	**WORTH FOUR FREE BOOKS PLUS A FREE SIMULATED PEARL HEART PENDANT**
🍒	🍒	🍒	**WORTH THREE FREE BOOKS**
⬤	⬤	⬤	**WORTH TWO FREE BOOKS**
🔔	🔔	🍒	**WORTH ONE FREE BOOK**

Offer limited to one per household and not valid to current Silhouette Romance™ subscribers. All orders subject to approval.

© 1990 HARLEQUIN ENTERPRISES LIMITED   PRINTED IN U.S.A.

DETACH AND MAIL CARD TODAY

Experience the dark p... deadly pleasures of th... by Jenna M...

"A wonderful blend of fantasy, romance, and intoxicating adventure, wickedly spiced with danger."

—Gena Showalter, *New York Times* bestselling author

"Maclaine's attention to detail and description brings this sexy, adventurous paranormal romance to life…Clever Cin matches sass and bravery with an innocence and vulnerability that will allow her to grow and develop through what promises to be a highly entertaining series."

—*Publishers Weekly*

"An imaginative new series…With danger omnipresent, compelling characters keep the story lively and the relationships intriguing. Here's to the next installment."

—*Romantic Times*

"I enjoyed the hero, the heroine, the plot, the secondary characters, the setting, the pacing…you name it, I liked it. Do yourself a favor…if you're looking for something different in the paranormal or historical romance arena, pick up *Wages of Sin*."

—*Good Reads Reviews*

MORE…

This is a work of fiction. All of the characters, organizations, and events portrayed in this novel are either products of the author's imagination or are used fictitiously.

BOUND BY SIN

Copyright © 2010 by Jenna Maclaine.

For information address St. Martin's Press, 175 Fifth Avenue, New York, NY 10010.

ISBN: 978-0-312-94618-0

Printed in the United States of America

St. Martin's Paperbacks edition / January 2010

St. Martin's Paperbacks are published by St. Martin's Press, 175 Fifth Avenue, New York, NY 10010.

10 9 8 7 6 5 4 3 2 1

BOUND
BY SIN

Jenna Maclaine

St. Martin's Paperbacks

Introduction

The choice of theme

Had Hardy known in 1874 what a success *Far from the Madding Crowd* was to prove, his next novel would certainly have been a 'woodland story'. As he did not know in what direction his talent lay, and did not wish to be regarded as merely another writer of rural novels, he decided to try a new kind of subject. It was not until 1885 that he returned to the woodland story he had 'put aside'. He obviously thought of radical changes, for in November he wrote, 'Have gone back to my original plot for *The Woodlanders* after all. Am working from half-past ten a.m. to twelve p.m., to get my mind made up on the details.' This suggests that, though the main outline was preserved, Hardy introduced much that was new.

We have to go back to *Under the Greenwood Tree* and its title to find the origin of *The Woodlanders*. In both novels the plot hinges on the dilemma of an educated girl whose choice in marriage lies between an honest countryman, for whom she feels real affection and kinship, and a socially superior rival, to whom she is attracted for more superficial reasons. The title of the first was chosen by the publishers, Hardy's preference being 'The Mellstock Quire'. The selected title set Hardy thinking about the possibilities of a story based almost entirely in a woodland area of great appeal to him.

The appeal of the woodland story to Hardy

He was always very attached to his family, and as a boy loved to hear, from his mother and grandmother particularly, stories concerning his parents, their ancestors and the places where they had lived. *Under the Greenwood Tree* developed from tales he heard about his father and grandfather as string players at Stinsford church. The 'woodland story' which Hardy began to plan in 1874 was set in the country around his mother's birthplace. He loved it for its family associations and for its natural beauty. 'The stretch of country visible from the heights adjoining the nook herein described under the name of Little Hintock, cannot be regarded as inferior to any inland scenery of the sort in the west of England, or

11

perhaps anywhere in the kingdom,' he wrote in his first preface to *The Woodlanders*.

The natural world and human suffering

When the Hardy of 1874 thought of Shakespeare's song 'Under the greenwood tree', and particularly of the lines:

> Here shall he see
> No enemy
> But winter and rough weather

he must have had considerable reservations. He knew, as Tennyson had known, that Nature was 'red in tooth and claw'. *The Origin of Species* by Charles Darwin confirmed impressions which he had seen for himself on the heath and in the woodlands near his home at Higher Bockhampton. However beautiful the scene might appear to the casual observer, one didn't have to look far to find evidence of the struggle for existence and the survival of the fittest in plants and trees, insects and birds and animals. These aspects of nature are frequently presented in *The Woodlanders*, and very rarely in *Under the Greenwood Tree*, which in general is a humorous, light-hearted story.

In *The Woodlanders* the struggles and stresses of nature have their parallel in human affairs, so often are there forces at work which make the principal characters suffer. Whereas the heroine of *Under the Greenwood Tree* makes the right choice in marriage, the heroine of *The Woodlanders* does not. The first novel ends with the song of the nightingale and happy associations with the lines quoted above from Shakespeare's song. The bird which comments sarcastically on the first real hint of oncoming disaster for the heroine of the second is a bird of ill omen, the night-hawk with its 'coarse whirr'. At this juncture, Hardy adds, the time of nightingales is past.

A change of subject

It was with thoughts on these lines, and on the problem of unhappy marriages, that Hardy struggled towards the completion of his final plan for *The Woodlanders*, the first novel he wrote at Max Gate. The change from his previous novel, *The Mayor of Casterbridge*, could hardly have been greater. In place of a town setting we have one which is rural and sequestered; the emphasis is on love and marriage rather than on business

12

"A unique plot and setting, as well as a diverse and well developed cast of characters. Filled with danger, passion, and magic, *Wages of Sin* is sure to please fans of paranormal romance. I highly recommend it."

—*Romance Reviews Today*

"I am a particular fan of vampire stories in which vampires are defenders of humanity, to the point of slaying their own kind. Those books are few and far between, but when they come along, they tend to be quality and this is no exception. The author's ability to build a complex world where there is well defined good vs. evil makes her prose strong and vivid. Seeing how Dulcinea, or Cin as she comes to be called, evolves will be intriguing."

—*Huntress Reviews*

"A great love story…I can't wait to find out what happens next with The Righteous. A definite keeper!"

—*Night Owl Reviews*

ACKNOWLEDGMENTS

I'd like to take this opportunity to thank some people who perhaps have not gotten a mention in the acknowledgments of the previous books. They have helped me with storylines, character names, research, editing, or simply with moral support. With much appreciation I'd like to thank: my dogs (for keeping my feet warm while I write), Anna, Bill & Amy, Brian, Brianna, Callie, Carol, Caroline, Cecily, Charlie, Chris, Colin, Dana, Don, Donna, Freda, Heather, Jennifer K, Jennifer V, Jerry, Joyce, Kacey, Kait, Kerry, Kristen & Sam, Linda C, Linda R, Lynn, Marci & Randy, Marie S, Marie T, Misty, Natasha, Niki, Pat, Sarah & Channing, Shannon & Jeremy, Shannon S, Sheri, Tracy & David, Ulrike . . . and, as always, Mom & Dad.

To my friend Jamie, who got me started in this genre. And by that I mean she nagged me with author recommendations until I gave in, even though I kept telling her that "I don't read vampire books." Thanks for sticking in there, girl!

And to the late, great Kathryn Wright—my teacher and my friend. She opened doors to worlds I had never imagined, and she will always be greatly loved and missed.

for the latter but it was nice, on occasion, to drink from a willing donor—someone who wasn't a rapist, cutthroat, or thief who had the misfortune to accost the wrong woman, namely me, in a dark alley.

Buying blood certainly didn't carry with it the same thrill as hunting in the aforementioned dark alleys, but the drinking was undeniably more pleasant. Instead of a rank, filthy alley, tonight I was reclining on a chaise lounge in a private parlor that was sumptuously decorated in silks and satins of varying shades of blue. The young man whose blood I had purchased was no ruffian smelling of sweat and gin. He was beautiful, blond, and shirtless—and perfectly willing to let me to sink my teeth into any vein of my choosing. Yes, quite a departure from my usual fare.

I looked at the young man again as he silently ran his fingers through my long, curling, blood-red hair. He was undeniably lovely but I knew that I could never grow accustomed to drinking from a blood whore on a regular basis. Many vampires do but, to me, it was rather like feeding a tiger in a cage. The tiger will live, it may even thrive, but it will always miss the hunt. Sometimes, however, a change of pace was nice and the vampire brothels were convenient.

The blood whores actually commanded quite a lucrative trade. Even in the smallest cities, vampire brothels are on par with the most exclusive houses of prostitution in Paris or London. Vampires, as a rule, have expensive

CHAPTER 1

There is darkness inside all of us, though mine is more dangerous than most. Still, we all have it—that part of our soul that is irreparably damaged by the very trials and tribulations of life. We are what we are because of it, or perhaps in spite of it. Some use it as a shield to hide behind, others as an excuse to do unconscionable things. But, truly, the darkness is simply a piece of the whole, neither good nor evil unless you make it so. It took a witch, a war, and a voodoo queen to teach me that.

Le Havre, France 1862

The House of the Crescent Moon was a brothel where the blood whores plied their trade. For a few coins a vampire could get a quick meal. For a few more, one could buy an evening's entertainment. I had no need taste and are willing to pay for the luxuries these houses provide. The men and women who serve in such places are the most beautiful creatures that money can buy. And why wouldn't they be? If selling your body was your chosen profession, you couldn't find a better place to do it. The houses were magnificently well-appointed, the money they made was ten times better than what they could have earned in even the best human brothels, vampires carry no diseases, and the clientele was . . . well, suffice it to say that there are humans who would pay a high price for the pleasures to be found in a vampire's bed.

Thoughts of such passions made me turn my attention from my human to the vampire lounging on a sofa across the parlor. I watched as his sensual lips moved against the lovely, pale throat of a buxom brunette, searching for the perfect spot to strike. She clung to him, her head thrown back, and when his teeth slid into her flesh she clutched his dark blond hair and let out a moan of pleasure. I felt a twinge of jealousy at the sight. He was my husband, after all.

Let her enjoy it while she can, I thought.

As if he sensed my gaze on him, Michael looked up. His need for blood almost quenched, there was now lust in his eyes. And it was directed at me. He pulled back from the brunette's neck and a trail of crimson blood flowed down her white skin. Never taking his gaze from me, Michael caught the trickle of blood on his tongue and licked his way up the side of her throat in one long stroke. A shudder ran through me as I imagined taking him back to the hotel and letting him fulfill the promise that was evident in that one smoldering look.

"Come to me," I said to my human.

The young man sat up and I rolled onto my back, stretching out across the velvet-upholstered chaise. He leaned over me and I admired the way the muscles in his arms and shoulders tightened as he moved closer, exposing his neck. I stared into his chocolate brown eyes until I felt the familiar click in my head that meant he was now under my control.

You could certainly drink without bespelling a human but I didn't want him to feel the pain of my bite, only the pleasure. When you take someone's blood you make a mental connection with them, sharing their thoughts and feelings. It could be horrifying, pleasant, or downright erotic, depending on whom you were drinking from and to what degree you allowed that connection. I think of it as a door inside my head and I control how far I open it. Considering the caliber of men whose blood I generally took, I was used to keeping that door firmly closed. When I was a young vampire I'd learned very quickly that I didn't want to know what went on inside their minds.

Tonight, though, was different, and I thought it only polite to allow this human to experience some measure of the satisfaction I felt in drinking from him. I opened the door in my head, wanting him to feel what I felt as his hot blood poured down my throat and filled me with life. I was not prepared for the reciprocating emotions and images I received from him.

Hot pleasure rolled over me in waves and I was aware of him moving between my legs, pushing against me. As I drank from him, I closed my eyes and was overwhelmed with flashes of what he was thinking. He was imagining me on top of him, moving down his naked body with the cat-like grace of a vampire, parting his legs and sinking my teeth into his femoral artery. I quickly severed the connection, pulling away as he threw back his head and shuddered in rapture against me. I let out a shaky breath as he looked down at me with glazed eyes.

"Buy me for the night," he pleaded. "Let me make love to you."

Suddenly his weight was pulled from me and Michael was standing between us. My husband's blue eyes glittered and his sharp cheekbones seemed even more pronounced when he clenched his jaw that way. I smiled up at him, my body humming with excitement at the predatory look on his face.

"Sorry, boy," my husband said sharply as he held his hand out to me. "The lass has other plans tonight."

I placed my hand in his and let him pull me up from the chaise. When I'd gained my feet he snaked one strong arm around my waist and pulled me against his body.

"Tonight and every other night," I promised.

He kissed me swiftly. "For eternity, *mo ghraidh*," he whispered against my lips.

As we left the house I turned my face into the cool breeze, which carried with it the salty scent of the ocean. It was a clear, crisp night and the Hotel Frascati was a few blocks away. It seemed longer, though, with Michael whispering naughty things in my ear every few minutes. I was strolling along, happily contemplating the rest of my evening, when my vision began to blur and a sharp buzzing sound took up residence in my head.

"Dear Goddess," I mumbled, stopping short and pressing the heels of my hands to my eyes.

"What's wrong?" Michael asked.

"I don't know," I replied. "It feels like there's a nest of bees in my head."

I stumbled backward, as if I could somehow get away from the sound.

Michael grasped my upper arms to steady me. "Is it the blood?" he asked worriedly. "Was he tainted?"

"I don't think so," I replied, shaking my head as I tried to clear the buzzing sound from it. I'd often fed from drunks and several varieties of drug addicts. The aftereffects of taking in tainted blood varied, but you could always tell if a human was . . . polluted in any way . . . the minute their blood hit your tongue.

I pulled away from Michael and staggered off the sidewalk. I had the feeling that if I could keep moving

I could somehow dislodge that horrible sound. Michael plunged into the street after me, catching my arm and pulling me back just before I walked in front of an oncoming carriage. I hadn't even heard the rumble of the wheels on the cobblestones over the racket that was in my head. As I stood in his arms, facing the opposite side of the street, the sound lessened.

"I'll hail a carriage and we'll drive back to the hotel," Michael said.

He put his arm around my shoulders and began to steer me back onto the sidewalk in the direction we'd been headed. The buzzing sound returned, violently. I stopped again and glanced across the street. Grabbing Michael's hand, I looked both ways and marched across the street.

Better, I thought. *This is better.*

"Michael, what lies in that direction?" I asked, pointing to the darkened row of shops lining the street in front of me.

"The harbor is in that direction," he replied. "Why?"

I pinched the bridge of my nose between my fingers. "When I performed the summoning spell that brought you to me when we first met . . . what did it feel like?"

Michael frowned and then the tension eased from his body as he realized what was happening. "It felt exactly like a nest of bees in my head and it only stopped when I went in the direction that would take me to you."

"I didn't know what it would feel like," I said. "I'm so sorry to have put you through this."

Michael cupped my face with his hands. "Don't ever apologize for that. It brought me to you, did it not?"

I smiled up at him, able to think more clearly now that I knew I wasn't losing my mind. "I suppose we must go to the harbor," I said.

Michael shook his head. "I am not running after some witch powerful enough to do this to you without first knowing where we're going and why."

He was right about that. At this point I'd have run headlong into no telling what sort of danger, just to get this infernal buzzing to stop.

"Let's just go have a look," I suggested. "First we'll see where the magic wants me to go."

A muscled ticked in Michael's jaw but he finally relented and hailed a carriage to take us to the docks. The harbor was filled with all manner of vessels, from small fishing boats to larger steamships. I appreciated the convenience of the new steamships but, in my opinion, nothing could match the grace and beauty of a sailing vessel. I laid my head on Michael's shoulder and closed my eyes as I nestled against his chest. He put his arms around me and we sat in silence as the carriage lumbered along. The buzzing, which had diminished from a dull roar to a soft hum the closer we'd gotten to the harbor, suddenly softened until I could barely hear it at all.

"Here," I said and Michael rapped on the roof of the carriage. The driver brought the conveyance to an abrupt halt and I peered out the window, taking in the sleek lines and tall masts of the ship that someone's magic wanted me to board.

A sailor passed by the carriage, an Englishman by the sound of his voice as he softly sang a rather vulgar ditty.

"Pardon me," I called out to him. "Do you know this ship?"

"Aye, miss," he replied, smiling at the sound of my English accent. "That's the *Charlotte Ann*."

"Where is she bound?" I asked.

"London on the next tide, miss," he answered.

I thanked him and sat back with a sigh. "Well, that's a relief," I said. "We should return to the Frascati and find Devlin and Justine."

Michael frowned. "Cin, just because that ship is headed for London doesn't necessarily mean whoever is summoning you is a friend."

"You're right, of course. But how many witches do you think there are in Britain who would not only work a spell to summon me specifically, but are also powerful enough to do it?" I gazed out at the silent harbor, the water silver in the moonlight, and keenly felt the pull of the spell. "Someone is calling me home."

CHAPTER 2

London

It felt good to be home, if for no other reason than that maddening buzzing grew weaker the closer I got to Ravenworth. I no longer needed the humming compass in my head to gauge my direction. Now that I was back in England the magic that called to me was stronger; it was an inexorable pull that drew me home. I knew where I needed to go. What bothered me was why.

It had been nearly a year since I'd been back to see Fiona. She was an old woman now, nearly fifty years having passed since that autumn when I was turned. To save us all from a demon bent on destroying the world, I had become a vampire. I had given up my life so that my friends would live. Fiona had inherited my property and part of my fortune, and had gone on to have the life I should have had.

They're all gone now, all but Fiona and Archie, I thought sadly as I watched the scenery change outside the carriage window, the tall buildings of the city giving way to more pastoral scenes.

Mr. Pendergrass, who had owned the apothecary shop in London and had been so helpful to a young witch unsure of her power, had died of old age two years after my turning. Fiona's mother, Lady Bascombe, had succumbed to influenza twenty years ago. Even my Aunt Maggie had been gone for nearly a decade now. Archie, who had been Mr. Pendergrass's apprentice and who still owned the apothecary shop, and Fiona were the only ties I had left to my human life.

I ran my fingers absently over the smooth skin of my cheek and then down through my dark red curls. The lines of age would never mar my face; silver would never streak my hair. I would forever look twenty-two, exactly as I had in the autumn of 1815 when I had died and been reborn as a vampire.

"I don't even need to ask what you're thinking, lass," Michael said as he leaned across the carriage and scooped me up, settling me comfortably in his lap.

I rested my head in the crook of his neck and breathed in the scent of him. "I'm worried about Fiona," I said. "She looked so frail when we were last here."

"She is nearly seventy now, *mo ghraidh*," he said softly. "But she seemed in good spirits."

I shook my head. "I don't understand why I'm being summoned home and, moreover, who would be powerful enough to do it. Fiona has no magic."

"Don't worry so," Michael said. "We'll be at Ravenworth in a few hours and then we'll see."

Ravenworth, I thought as I closed my eyes and settled against the hard wall of Michael's chest. I wondered, when they were all gone, if it would still feel like home.

All three stories of Ravenworth Hall were lit up like a beacon in the night. It was a welcoming sight, even if the reason I was here still bothered me. Before Devlin had the chance to pull the horses to a complete stop, I flung the carriage door open and bounded to the ground. I heard Justine call my name as I rushed up the front steps. Without bothering to knock, I opened the door and stepped into the foyer. The house was silent and empty except for the dark gray cat with white markings that sat on the steps of the grand staircase and watched me with interest.

I rushed through the house, knowing instinctively where a witch would cast such a spell. I knew because I had done it once myself. When I reached the closed double doors of the ballroom I paused, waiting for the others to catch up to me. Glancing behind me at my companions, I shook my head and smiled. I hoped that

Fiona had prepared the witch for the sight of us because we looked like what we were—The Righteous, four of the most feared vampires in the world.

My masculine attire perhaps made me look more threatening, though that hadn't been my intention. It wasn't that I didn't have trunks full of beautiful dresses; it was simply that I preferred to wear my boots and breeches these days, if I could. Unlike the less complicated fashions of my youth, today's gowns with their corsets, crinolines, hoops, and petticoats required more dressing time than I thought was reasonable. Tonight I was wearing all black, from my silk pirate's shirt with its falls of lace, to my leather breeches and boots. My pale skin and blood-red hair made a startling contrast against the dark garments. Dressed like this I would never be mistaken for what I once was, a viscount's daughter. I was now Cin Craven, the Red Witch of the Righteous, though some simply called me the Devil's Witch in deference to Devlin, the leader of our group.

I couldn't help but feel his massive presence behind me, nearly six and a half feet of solid muscle. Devlin, the Dark Lord, with his black hair and eyes, his chiseled features, had once been one of Edward III's champions. He truly had been a knight in shining armor and I would always think of him as such. When I had been a scared human, hunted by vampires, he had helped save me.

Justine moved silently to my left. She was my closest

friend and Devlin's consort. The vampires called her the Devil's Justice, and not without reason. She had a face and figure that would turn any man's head, but that was only part of her appeal. The former courtesan was sex and danger incarnate—a beautiful woman who was never without a weapon. Even now I wondered how many blades were hidden beneath the voluminous folds of her cloak.

Michael's hand reached out to touch my shoulder and I turned my head. The Devil's Archangel they called him, for none in the vampire nation could match his skill with a sword. He nodded toward the closed doors of the ballroom and my mind briefly raced back to the last time a summoning spell had been worked in that room.

I remembered well the look on his face as he'd shoved open the terrace doors and his eyes had met mine. "*Witch*," he'd growled in frustration, and I smiled at the memory. Though they'd initially been irritated at my summoning, the three of them had done everything in their power to help me. I looked back at Michael, my husband, my heart, and soul. Perhaps things had not turned out as any of us had expected, but he truly had saved me. I laid my hands on the ballroom doors.

And it had all started here, just like this, I thought.

Taking a deep breath, I pushed open the massive double doors and strode inside, the clicking of my heels echoing sharply in the empty, cavernous room.

CHAPTER 3

Well, the room wasn't entirely empty. Two women stood at the far end, in front of the circle of candles that had been laid out for the summoning spell. For a moment my steps faltered and my breath caught in my throat.

Aunt Maggie.

Michael had often said that my aunt was too mean to die. I believe his phrase was, "Heaven wouldn't have her and hell would be afraid she'd take over." But she had died, hadn't she? Ten years ago next spring. I walked slowly to the woman until I was standing mere inches from her. Without speaking, I simply stared. By the Goddess, she looked just like Maggie had the last time I'd seen her, back in '28. The same gray hair and faintly lined features, the same iron will shining through her beautiful cornflower blue eyes.

"You're the very image of my Aunt Maggie," I whispered.

The woman blinked and then smiled sadly. "I am her granddaughter and your second cousin. My name is Raina Macgregor Mahone."

"Raina," I murmured. "Yes, I remember you. Mahone? You married Tristan, then?"

Tristan Mahone was a necromancer who had once caused considerable trouble for the vampires of Edinburgh.

She nodded. "I did."

"Is he . . . here?" I asked.

She shook her head and I could feel the tension ease from all the vampires in the room, myself included.

"I wish he were," she said, "but, as you know, he gave his word never to leave Glen Gregor."

I nodded. "I'm glad he's kept his promise."

Raina shrugged. "Having the king and queen of the vampires angry with you is very powerful motivation."

Indeed, I thought. MacLeod and Marrakesh had promised him swift death if he ever set foot on their lands again.

I turned to the other woman in the room.

"Hello, Janet," I said to Fiona's only daughter.

"Welcome home, Cin," she replied with a genuinely warm smile.

Gods, she certainly had the look of her mother.

"Which begs the question, why am I home?" I asked, turning back to Raina. "Only an extremely powerful witch could have called me here from France. I assume that would be you. Now I'd like for you to tell me why."

Raina swallowed hard and for the first time I noticed the fear in her eyes. "My youngest daughter is in grave danger," she said. "I need your help."

I closed my eyes and might have laughed if it hadn't been completely inappropriate. When I had been a young, scared human I had stood exactly where she was and cast a spell to call The Righteous to my aid. The irony was not lost on me.

I opened my eyes and looked back at Raina. I wondered what my aunt, who had wholeheartedly disapproved of vampires in general and me in particular, would have thought of her granddaughter asking for my help.

"I'll do whatever I can," I replied. "But first I'd like to see Fiona."

CHAPTER 4

I stood in Ravenworth's small chapel, staring numbly at the plaque in front of me. Reaching out with one shaking hand, I traced the letters with my fingers.

FIONA MACKENZIE BASCOMBE

1793–1861

BELOVED WIFE, MOTHER, AND FRIEND

I pressed my other hand to my chest, feeling as though there were a gaping hole there that would never be filled. I'd always known this day would come, but it was still hard to believe that she was truly gone. Leaning forward, I rested my forehead against the cold stone wall. The soft whisper of Janet's skirts broke the silence as she moved up behind me, placing her hands gently on my shoulders.

"I loved her like a sister," I said brokenly.

"And she loved you just the same," Janet replied.

"Why didn't she tell me she was sick?" I asked. "I would have stayed."

"She didn't want you to have to watch her die, Cin. She said that she remembered how hard her mother's death was on you and she wouldn't put you through that again."

I closed my eyes, remembering the night that Fiona had smuggled me into her mother's bedroom on the neighboring estate, so that I could say goodbye. Jane Mackenzie Bascombe had contracted a particularly violent strain of influenza and it had been torture to see her lying there, just a few ragged breaths away from death. She had always been so strong and vibrant, the backbone of our family. She'd been my nanny when I was a child and later our housekeeper, but the inheritance I'd left Fiona upon my "death" had bought them both respectability and good marriages.

"Cin?" Janet said and I realized that I hadn't heard a word she'd been saying.

"Was she scared?" I asked.

"Of dying?"

I nodded.

"No," Janet replied. "She wasn't scared. She was very tired . . . and she was ready."

I smiled sadly. "Of course she wouldn't be scared. Even when we were being hunted by vampires she was so brave and fearless. I wish you could have seen her back then, Janet. Do you know she once cracked me over the head with a vase and tied me to a chair? All in an effort to protect me from myself, you understand, but I think she enjoyed it just a little too much."

Janet laughed. "Yes, I can very well imagine her doing that."

"She had a warrior's heart."

"And an excellent sense of humor," Janet said. "Mother told me that if you got too morose I should ask you what you thought of the new addition to your own marker."

I had avoided looking in that direction. Visiting the final resting place of a friend is one thing, but visiting your own grave is just morbid. I hadn't wanted anything elaborate, just a simple plaque with my name and dates of birth and death. I turned my head slightly to the left and glanced at the spot next to Fiona's where my empty casket rested beneath the ground. It had always said:

DULCINEA MACGREGOR CRAVEN

1793–1815

However, at some point over the years Fiona had added:

SHE WILL LIVE FOREVER

IN OUR HEARTS

The script of the last line was so small that it was hard to read, even for me, in the dark chapel. I threw my head back and laughed and, somewhere, I knew Fiona was laughing with me.

CHAPTER 5

We all assembled in what had formerly been known as the green drawing room. Several years ago Janet had redecorated many of the rooms in the house and the green drawing room was now predominantly peach with white moldings and accents of mint green. The new color scheme was lovely but tonight it made my heart ache, just a little. It seemed that everything around me was changing while I remained the same. *Well, one thing hasn't changed*, I thought as I stared at the portrait Michael had painted of me shortly after I'd become a vampire. *I still hate that painting.* And for some unfathomable reason Janet had decided to move it from my bedroom and hang it next to the portraits of Rainy Macgregor and great-grandmother Charlotte.

Wearily, I sat down on one of the newly upholstered chairs. Justine walked up behind me and laid her hand on my shoulder in a comforting gesture. I reached up and placed mine over hers. She knew what I was feeling right now because she had been there. Over 130 years ago Justine had buried her only sister. She had warned me long ago that this day would come. When I was still human and considering the ramifications of becoming a vampire, she'd told me that I would have to be strong enough to watch those I loved die while I remained young forever. At the time, though, the prospect of that happening had seemed such a long way off.

"Cin, I want to thank you for helping me," Raina said, dragging my attention back to the situation at hand.

I nodded. "Even if she weren't family, I do owe you a debt," I replied.

She frowned, looking at me as though she didn't comprehend my meaning.

"Back in '28 when Tristan was in Edinburgh foolishly helping Belladonna try to steal the queen's throne, you sent Drummond to help me," I explained. "A necromancer has power over the dead, but not over a werewolf. Drummond quite handily saved the day. If you hadn't insisted he come to Edinburgh, there's no telling what might have happened to us, or Aunt Maggie."

Before Raina could reply, Devlin interrupted. "Please tell us what's happened here," he said. "From the beginning."

Raina turned her attention to him and nodded. "Claire is my youngest," she explained. "I know that mothers aren't supposed to have favorites among their children, but Claire has always been special to me. Perhaps it's because she just required so much attention. From the day she was born, trouble has followed that child. Nearly every day of her life there's some new drama and, well, things happen to her that just don't happen to other people. If she said she was late for supper because she was swimming with kelpies in the loch, I'd believe her."

We must have had similar looks of skepticism on our faces because Raina added, "Do you want an example? The summer she turned seven Claire wandered off and got lost in the hills. My magic couldn't find her and I feared that she was dead. We searched for two days before we happened upon her, frolicking in a small glen with some rabbits and a baby deer while the doe patiently stood guard. She was clean, didn't seem to be hungry or thirsty, and told us fantastic tales of the faerie lady who had watched over her. That is not an isolated incident. It's only one story out of many.

"Claire is well-loved in Glen Gregor but the people watch her with a wary eye, as if she were a changeling child. She has such a good heart, but most people only see her eccentricities. It was not unreasonable for her father and me to think that she might never marry. All I ever wanted for her was that she one day find a man who would love her and take care of her, a man who would be strong enough to share her life. She thought she'd found that man in Alastair Gordon, the new gamekeeper I hired when she was seventeen."

Raina closed her eyes and shook her head.

"I take it he was not all you'd hoped he would be?" I asked.

Raina's mouth settled into a grim line. "He was not. Oh, he was a bonny lad and quite charming as well. He came to Glen Gregor with excellent recommendations and I didn't have a single cause to worry about his character that first year he worked for us. Claire completely lost her head over the boy, of course. We all thought he loved her too. And maybe he did, in his own way. But scarcely a month after they were wed I visited Claire and found a large purple bruise on her cheek. She laughed it off, saying that she'd tripped over a chicken and fallen against the well."

I arched a brow at her.

"I know, I know," Raina said with a sigh. "But you have to understand that, though she's rarely injured, Claire is incredibly accident prone. Especially as a child, if there was a river to fall into or a tree to fall out of, she'd find it. And her tale was just so detailed and convincing that I believed her. Over the next few months, however, she seemed to acquire bumps and bruises at an astonishing rate and I began to fear that Alastair was beating her."

"Was he?" Michael asked in a cold voice.

I glanced up at him. His jaw was clenched in anger, his blue eyes as hard as steel. My husband could not abide a man who would strike a woman.

"Oh, yes," Raina said. "Alastair was so sweet and courteous to her in public, so Tristan and I hid outside their house one night, watching, waiting to see how he treated her when no one was looking. He was late coming in from the hills. It was nearly midnight when he finally stumbled through his front door, drunk as a fish, and demanded to know why his supper wasn't hot and waiting on the table. He'd split her lip open and bloodied her nose by the time Tris broke the door down."

"I'd have killed the bastard," Devlin growled. "But what did you do?"

Raina looked at him for a long moment, then continued. "Tristan dragged him outside and beat him bloody. And when he was finished, I shot Alastair Gordon through the heart."

Janet gasped. "Raina!"

Raina shrugged, as if it were of little consequence. "We told everyone that he'd been waylaid by poachers in the hills."

"But a gunshot at night would have been heard in the village, *non*?" Justine asked.

"I'm sure it was. No one really believed the story about the poachers, anyway. There was no way to hide Claire's broken nose, two black eyes, and cut lip at the funeral."

"Weren't you afraid someone would tell the authorities that you'd murdered a man?" Janet asked, her eyes wide with astonishment.

I knew the answer to that question already. Raina turned to Janet, arching one silver brow. She looked so much like Maggie in that moment—the same regal bearing, the same utter confidence in her own power—that I could almost believe it was my aunt sitting in front of me.

"I am the Macgregor Witch," Raina said. "In Glen Gregor, my will is law. No one would question it."

And that was that. Glen Gregor was our family estate in Scotland. It had been established by my English great-grandfather as a refuge for my Scottish relatives after Bonnie Prince Charlie's defeat at Culloden. Over time, those who lived in the castle and those who populated the village had evolved into something of a voluntary feudal society. For generations the eldest female of my family, the one thought to possess the strongest of our hereditary magic, had been the matriarch of the glen. As isolated as they were in the wild western highlands of Scotland, the Macgregor Witch had always ruled with the authority of a queen.

"The only reason I bring up Alastair Gordon is to explain the circumstances of our being in London. It took me two years to undo the damage that man did to Claire in a few short months of marriage. Finally, this past autumn she began to seem like her old self again. I thought a trip to London for the Season would be a wonderful experience for her so I rented a house and brought her down just after Christmas. She was a little quiet and preferred to stay in more than I expected she would, but I attributed that to the fact that London can be a bit frightening and overwhelming when you've lived your entire life in sleepy little Glen Gregor. For the most part we had a grand time over the next two months, shopping and attending many musicales, teas, and balls."

"And then what happened?" I asked.

Raina closed her eyes and leaned back in her chair. "And then Claire was kidnapped," she said softly.

CHAPTER 6

"I went to wake her one morning," Raina said. "Well, it was afternoon actually, since we'd been out late at a ball. She wasn't in her room. He must have taken her directly out of the country because I tried a location spell and I couldn't find her. My magic isn't strong enough," she said, looking at me, "but yours might be."

I nodded. "All right. I'll certainly be glad to give it a try. But Raina, you said 'he' took her. Do you know who abducted her?"

Raina's eyes narrowed. "I have a fairly good idea. It was that bloody American, Adrien Boucher."

Justine cocked her head to one side. "This is a French name," she said.

"His family is French, from Louisiana I believe, but I remember him saying that he no longer lives there. Obviously, now I wish I'd paid more attention to him. We met him at several parties when we first arrived in town and it was rumored that he was in England to raise money for the secessionist cause. The Americans are having a civil war, you know."

I nodded. "Yes, I still read the newspapers. But if his purpose in coming to England was to raise money, why abduct Claire and leave so suddenly? Has there been a ransom demand?"

"No," Raina replied. "I'm sure it all has to do with that urn, though I can't believe it was that valuable."

I closed my eyes. My head was beginning to pound. "What urn?" I asked patiently.

Raina looked at me blankly for a moment. "Oh, right, I haven't yet told you about the urn. Forgive me, as you can imagine I'm a little scattered right now. On one of our first excursions in town, Claire and I ventured into an antiquities shop. While I was admiring several very nice pieces of silver, Claire struck up a conversation with a young widow who had come to the shop to sell some of her late husband's belongings. Apparently the man had been some sort of archaeologist and possessed many artifacts he'd brought back from Greece. Claire has always had a keen love of Greek and Roman mythology, so she and the young lady talked for quite some time on the subject while the proprietor decided which items he wished to purchase. Claire particularly admired this rather dreadful-looking urn and the widow made her a gift of it. I offered repeatedly to pay her for it, since it was obvious she was in need of the funds, else why would she be there? She would have none of it, though, and insisted that Claire keep the urn. Other than Claire herself, it was the only thing missing from her room."

Devlin stood and began pacing. "Why would a man who risked running the blockades to leave America and come to England to raise money for a war, steal a girl and a piece of antique crockery and leave without what he came for? If the urn had any real value, the widow of an archaeologist would surely know it and would not have just given it away."

"I do not believe we can assume that. Not all women show an interest in their husband's work," Justine pointed out. "Perhaps she did not know what she had?"

I turned to Raina. "Ah, but did Adrien Boucher know what she had?"

"Yes," Raina replied slowly. "I think he did. As I said, we'd crossed paths with Boucher several times and Claire enjoyed conversing with him because she said he talked to her as if she had a brain in her head. Claire had grown very weary of the usual London gentlemen who saw nothing but her pretty face. One evening, shortly after she acquired the urn, she told Boucher about it. He came to call on her a few days later and I chaperoned, of course, but he seemed to have no interest in her, only in that urn. Claire brought it down from her bedroom and they talked at great length about what the markings meant. Boucher offered to buy it from her but she refused."

"So he came under the cover of darkness and took it anyway," Michael stated.

"Not directly," Raina said. "Over the next month or so he offered to purchase it on several more occasions. I have no proof that he took her, but no one has seen him in London since Claire disappeared."

"But why take Claire *and* the urn?" Michael asked.

"Perhaps she caught him stealing it and he took her so that she wouldn't wake the whole household," I suggested. "It would buy him time to get away."

"There are easier ways of silencing someone," Devlin said softly and with great meaning.

He was right, of course. Boucher could have killed her, or tied her up and gagged her. Either would have been much easier than taking a girl against her will through London, to the docks, and onto a ship without raising suspicion. No, for some reason he wanted the urn *and* Claire.

Raina sighed in frustration. "By Danu, I wish that widow had never given her the blasted urn in the first place."

I suddenly had a sinking feeling in the pit of my stomach. "Raina, what did the woman look like?"

Raina looked confused as to why I would ask such a thing, but she answered the question. "She was tall and slender with glossy black hair and eyes to match. High

cheekbones, square jaw, full lips. She was quite strik-
ing, really."

I groaned and leaned back in my chair.

Yes, she is, I thought. *As beautiful as a goddess
should be, and twice as manipulative.*

CHAPTER 7

I stood at the dining room table and unrolled a large map of the world that Raina had found in the library. As she tacked the corners down with silver candlesticks, I looked at the map, thinking of all the places Boucher could have taken Claire. I hoped that Raina's spell would find her. My magic worked a bit differently than that of the rest of my family and, for me, spellcasting was often a disaster. I flicked my fingers toward the candles and the wicks caught fire, flaring up dramatically before settling down to a nice, steady glow.

A loud thump, followed by Devlin's rather colorful cursing and Justine's hearty laughter, drew my attention to the hall. They were moving our trunks from the carriage into our rooms for the night. I closed the doors to the dining room, muffling the distracting sounds, and turned back to Raina.

"Before we begin, will you tell me how the spell works?" I asked.

"Have you never done a location spell before?" Raina asked, surprised.

I shrugged. "My magic tends to be a bit more active," I replied.

To illustrate my point I conjured a ball of pure magic in my hand, the small orb glowing and pulsating with iridescent gold light. I snapped my fingers and the ball disappeared. Raina's eyes widened briefly in amazement and then she smiled.

"This will work," she said. "With that kind of power, it has to."

She walked around to the other side of the table and I moved to stand across from her, the map between us.

"There are different ways to find things," she said. "If I were home, searching for something that would likely be found in a place that was familiar to me, I might use a pool of still water to call forth an image of the missing object's location. Since Claire is undoubtedly someplace I've never been before, that's hardly going to be helpful. The second option is what I used when I found you in Edinburgh all those years ago. For that, we need a map and an object belonging to the person we're seeking."

Raina reached into the pocket of her skirt and pulled out a small pearl earring. "This is Claire's," she said and placed it on the map. "Now, there are the herbs and the invocation and—"

And this is why I hated spellcraft. I didn't have the patience for it. I reached across the table and grasped Raina's hands in mine, placing her palms flat at the outer edges of the map with mine resting on top of hers. I closed my eyes and summoned my magic.

It rose within me, calling to Raina's own magic like an old friend. She was my cousin and, no matter how differently our powers might manifest themselves, our magic all came from the same source, passed down in our blood for generations. I felt the stirring of Raina's power answering my own. She gasped as her magic poured from her body, lured by my call. My power took hers in, devouring it like the ocean swallowing the waters of a river, and yet Raina's magic was still there, mingling with mine. I felt the heady rush of power rise between us and I might have set it free, just to see what it would do, but Raina had overcome her momentary shock and her will held it in place. She positively vibrated with focus and concentration and I cracked my eyes open to see what our magic had wrought.

The pearl earring was spinning like a top, caught up in a vortex of golden light that swirled like the winds of a cyclone.

"Say the words now," I instructed Raina.

"Use this magic to help us see/That which has been

stolen from me/Across mountain, sand, or water/Show me where to find my daughter."

The earring shot across the map at such a great speed that I thought it might fly off the table entirely. But it stopped, and when it did our magic receded, its work done. Raina opened her eyes and pulled her shaking hands from under mine.

With a shuddering breath she said, "I don't think we needed quite that much power."

I shrugged and pointed to the map. "Perhaps not, but it worked."

We both leaned over and looked at where the earring rested. It was a small American island, one of many off the coast of Georgia. Raina sank dejectedly into one of the dining room chairs. I knew exactly how she felt. We had all been hoping for a different result. I sat down across from her and stared at the map, wondering how long it would take to find a ship whose captain was both willing and able to run a blockade during a war.

CHAPTER 8

Standing in the center of Ravenworth's winter garden, I closed my eyes and let the tension flow out of me. Tilting my head back, I reached out with my senses, listening to the stirring of the creatures of the night—and searching for one in particular.

"Morrigan," I called out. "You might as well show yourself. I know you're there."

There was a great flapping of wings and I opened my eyes to see a large raven perched on the high stone wall of the garden. Morrigan was a goddess of war and death, the fountainhead of the vampire race. It's said she often appears in the form of a raven. To me she had always been a beautiful young woman with hair the color of a raven's wing and long, black fingernails. I had long ago accepted the fact that she had a particular interest in molding me into the warrior she thought I should be. But that didn't mean I had to like it and the two of us at times butted heads over the matter. If the goddess had a hand in Claire's abduction, it was because of me. For that I felt a deep sense of guilt—and a large amount of anger.

"Really, Morrigan," I scoffed. "A faerie lady who watched over her while she was lost? A young widow who gifted her with something valuable enough to get her kidnapped? What the devil are you up to?"

The raven stared at me with its shiny black eyes and cocked its head to one side.

I stomped my foot. "Come down here and talk to me!"

Still she didn't move. Irritated, I conjured a ball of magic in the palm of my hand and hurled it at the raven. The bird shrieked and vanished just before the ball hit the stone with a flash of golden light. I looked around, wondering where she had disappeared to. A rushing flap of wings made me jerk my head up. The raven reappeared in midair just in front of me. Before I could get my hands up to shield my face, one long talon reached out and raked across my cheek. I put my hand to my face and came away with blood. The raven flew back to the wall and settled there, fluffing her wings and glaring at me. I looked at the blood on my fingers and inclined my head to her.

"Fine," I said. "We've proven that we can both be spiteful bitches. I suppose we could go at each other all night, but what's the point? I can't kill you and we both know you won't kill me. Why don't you just come down here and tell me what it is you want from me this time."

She shifted her weight from foot to foot, looking mildly impatient.

"All right, you want me to go to America, is that it?" I asked.

Her feathers ruffled and she settled calmly on the wall . . . and I swear the damned bird looked smug.

I sighed. "If you'd wanted me to go there, all you had to do was ask. You didn't have to involve an innocent young girl who is probably scared out of her mind right now."

The raven made a noise that on any other animal I would describe as a snort, and flew away. Exasperated, I threw one last ball of magic at the wall.

For the love of Danu, what would Morrigan want with a human girl like Claire?

CHAPTER 9

I walked back inside without an answer to my question. It would be dawn soon and I was tired and uneasy about what was to come. As I reached the grand staircase I noticed the gray and white cat perched on the newel post. Thinking that, with all that long hair, she must be a descendant of Prissy's, I stopped to pet her. Animals can generally sense the wrongness of the undead. Prissy, however, was never that smart and most of her descendants treated us vampires as any cat would a human. That is to say, as though we existed entirely for their benefit. The cat stood and stretched at my approach, letting out a rather demanding *meow*. I reached up to pet her and she eagerly rubbed her face against my hand.

"Well, hello," I said, smiling. "What's your name?"

"That's Not Harriette," Janet said from behind me.

I turned around. "I didn't say it was," I assured her. "What's her name?"

"She's Not Harriette," Janet reiterated.

"I understand she's not Harriette," I said slowly, wondering what had gotten into Janet. "Who is she?"

Janet laughed and shook her head. "No, Cin, her name is *Not Harriette*, though you're free to simply call her Harriette. The grandchildren got into an argument about what to name her. Lucy wanted Harriette but Jack was entirely against the idea. Every time Lucy would call the cat Harriette, Jack would yell, 'She's *not* Harriette!' Thus, the name."

I laughed as Janet plucked the cat from the newel post. She curled against Janet's chest, kneading and purring.

"She's one of Prissy's descendants?" I asked.

Janet nodded.

"She's beautiful," I remarked.

"And she knows it, too. I often find her sitting on my dressing table, making softly flirtatious feline noises to the pretty kitty in the mirror," Janet replied, and handed Harriette to me. "She's my favorite and travels with me wherever I go, but I think you need her more than I do tonight."

I looked down at the gray ball of fur, who meowed and butted her nose against mine. Smiling, I realized that I felt less tension than I had in days.

"I think I'll take you up on that offer, Janet," I said. "Thank you—for everything."

Michael was in bed when I walked into my room. I closed the door and put Harriette down. She immediately jumped up on the bed and strode arrogantly over to greet him, tail twitching. As I removed my clothes I listened to Michael talking softly to the cat. You never truly realize how much you enjoy the touch and comfort of an animal until it's gone. Unlike Ravenworth's cats, most animals will stay as far away from a vampire as possible.

I slid between the sheets and nestled against the warmth of Michael's body. The cat forgotten, he wrapped one arm around me and leaned over to kiss my lips. I lingered there for a moment, wishing I had the energy to follow where such kisses generally led. Harriette, as if sensing my mood, turned twice around on Michael's stomach and curled herself into a snug ball.

Michael glanced down at her. "At least this one doesn't want to sleep wrapped around my head like Prissy did," he said with a laugh.

I laid my head on his shoulder and ran my fingers over the smooth expanse of his chest.

"She's a smart girl," I said. "I can't think of any place I'd rather be than on top of you."

"If I thought that was an invitation, the cat would have to go," he teased.

"It could be," I murmured.

Michael brushed my hair back and kissed my forehead. "No, lass. You sleep now. We're going to have a long sea voyage ahead of us with little else to do but make love. Right now you're exhausted, worried, and a little angry, I think. Quite frankly," he said teasingly, "I don't believe you're capable of fully appreciating my considerable skills this morning."

I laughed. "I'm certain you're right about that."

"What worries you so about this trip?" he asked. "It's not as if the girl's been abducted by vampires. We go in and we take her back from a human. How much resistance can he possibly give us? I daresay the hardest part of the whole thing is going to be getting in and out of Savannah."

"It's Morrigan's involvement," I admitted. "Whenever she's around, things go horribly wrong. Venice, when I fought Gage and was infected with dark magic. Edinburgh, when I used that magic to incinerate all those vampires."

"Do I need to remind you that we'd all be dead if you hadn't done those things?" Michael asked softly.

"So you tell me every time we have this conversation. It doesn't change the fact that whenever she involves herself in my life I end up doing things I have no right to do. I've killed people, Michael. I've done things that we would execute any other vampire for doing. How is that all right?"

"Because none of the vampires we've executed have done what they did in service to the greater good. Your guilt can twist the past around however it likes, but the truth is that the world is a better place than it would have been had you not done these things."

"Perhaps," I agreed, thinking how many innocent people would have died if Edmund Gage had lived, or if that pack of rogues had succeeded in taking the city of Edinburgh. "But that doesn't mean I have to like it. What truly bothers me is that the more frightening my magic becomes, the happier it makes Morrigan. She says I'm to be some great warrior but what if I don't like the person she's making me into, Michael?"

"*Mo chridhe*," Michael chided. "Even Morrigan doesn't have that power. Our experiences lead us to *where* we are, they don't make us *who* we are. Only you can decide who it is you want to be."

I sighed and relaxed against him. "Have I told you yet today how much I love you?" I asked.

"Sleep now, lass. When you wake up you can show me."

CHAPTER 10

I woke to whiskers tickling my face. Opening my eyes, all I could see was gray fur and a pink nose coming directly at my face.

"*Meow*," Harriette said, and bumped her nose against mine.

"Do you have to go out?" I asked sleepily.

She made a happy cat sound and hopped off the bed. I got up and crossed the room to open the door, which she walked through without so much as a backward glance. *Cats*, I thought. A dog would have said thank you.

I leaned against the door and looked around the room. This was the bedroom I'd grown up in as a human. Fiona and I had played with our dolls in this room. We'd had tea parties and talked about the men we'd marry and what our lives would be like. I walked to the dressing table and absently ran my fingers over the back of the chair as I looked in the mirror. Fiona was gone now, yet my own reflection hadn't changed much at all from the day I'd stood right here, staring into this same mirror as I watched her lace me into my first corset.

Turning away, I looked at my bed and the man lying in it. This was the same bed where Fiona's mother had sung me to sleep as a child. It was the same bed where I had cried myself unconscious on the night my parents had died. This was where I had lost my virginity, and my life.

I closed my eyes. Now that Fiona was gone, the things about this house that had brought me so much comfort over the years only made me sad. I looked back at the bed, my gaze latching on to the one thing that was constant in my life. Michael. No matter how the world changed around me, he would always be there, and he would always love me.

He was stretched out on his back with one arm flung over his head. Ever so slowly, I slid the covers off of him. I didn't believe for a moment that he was still asleep, but he laid there with his eyes closed and let me enjoy the view. My gaze moved up and down the practically perfect lines of his naked body, wondering where to start. I smiled wickedly as one particular part of his anatomy stood up and volunteered.

I crawled gently across the bed, watching to see how long Michael was going to feign sleep. Propping myself on one elbow, I reached out and ran my fingertips up and down the length of his manhood. It leaped at my touch and I glanced back up at his face but his eyes were still closed, his features still as peaceful as a sleeping angel.

Devilishly, I arched one brow and smiled. I leaned over him, my breath hot on his sensitive skin, my lips so close but never touching him. Slowly I moved up the impressively hard length of him until my lips hovered just at the tip. I rolled my eyes up and watched his face as my tongue darted out to swirl several times around the head of his shaft before I drew him into my mouth.

With a low growl his eyes flew open and his hand shot out, gently grasping the back of my head, tangling his fingers in my scarlet curls. I moaned in satisfaction at the look on his face as I brought him pleasure with my mouth. I could do this for hours on end but Michael was rarely that patient. Indeed, within a few minutes he'd tossed me on my back and returned the favor until we were both wild with the need to finish.

"Now, Michael," I gasped. "Please now."

He spread my legs wide and plunged into me, throwing back his head with a groan of rapture. I slid my legs up until my ankles rested on his shoulders, and beckoned him to me. He leaned over and his lips met mine, his tongue moving with the rhythm of his body. At this angle the pleasure was so exquisite that if I hadn't already been dead I might have expired from the overwhelming feel of him moving so deeply, so tightly, within me.

Michael broke the kiss, his lips trailing across my cheek. "Come for me, lass," he whispered raggedly.

His words sent fresh shivers through me. "Not yet," I begged, not wanting it to end.

"Now," he growled. "Do it for me now."

And then he bit me. His teeth sank into the vein in my neck and my blood flowed into his mouth as he exploded inside me. As with any bite from a vampire, for a moment I could feel what he felt—the indescribable pleasure of his release. It drove me over the edge and I screamed his name as I followed him into that wondrous place where time stops and the only thing in the world that matters is the throbbing ecstasy of our joined bodies.

As he licked the blood from my skin, I eased my legs off his shoulders and wrapped them around his waist. Little tremors were still happily traveling through my body and I wasn't about to let him move until they'd stopped. He looked down at me and smiled. By the gods, he was so impossibly handsome that I often still marveled that he was mine.

"Have I told you yet today how much I love you?" he asked teasingly.

I chuckled and squeezed my legs tighter around him, drawing him closer. "Give me a few minutes," I said, "and you can show me. Again."

CHAPTER 11

An hour after sunset I stood alone in my room, checking one last time to make sure I hadn't left anything behind. Tonight we would go back to London and hope there was a Blood Cross ship in port that was willing to take us to America. The Blood Cross line was a shipping company owned and operated by a vampire named Sinclair. Back in '28 Sinclair's wife, Belladonna, had left him and run off to Edinburgh, dragging with her a young and impressionable human necromancer named Tristan Mahone. Bel's attempt to depose the vampire Queen of the Western Lands had resulted in banishment for them both: Bel to Sinclair's island in the Caribbean, and Tristan to Glen Gregor. And now here I stood, hoping that one of Sinclair's ships would take me across an ocean to rescue Tristan's daughter. I laughed softly at the irony of that.

"Michael and Devlin are just loading the trunks onto the coach," Janet said softly from the doorway.

Looking up sharply from my reverie, I found her and Raina waiting patiently for me. I walked to Raina and took her hands in mine.

"I will bring her back safely," I said. "I promise."

She nodded as if she wanted to believe me, but her eyes told a different tale. "I'm afraid for her, Cin. I'm afraid of what he might have done to her. She has to be terrified. She's only twenty-one and so fragile right now, especially where men are concerned."

"She's a Macgregor woman," I said. "When times are tough, we find the strength we need to survive."

Raina smiled sadly. "I guess we do at that."

"Will you be coming back in the summer, Cin?" Janet asked, referring to my yearly visits to Ravenworth.

I looked at her and Raina, the two of them standing there looking so much like two other women I had loved and lost, and it was almost more than I could bear.

"I honestly don't know," I answered, then walked over to Janet and hugged her tightly. "I love you, my girl. I have loved you and your brothers from the moment you came into this world, never forget that. But right now it hurts me to be here and I don't know when that hurt will lessen."

"I understand," she said softly. "I will miss you, Cin, but you know that this is your home and you're always welcome here."

I turned and took one last look, soaking in the memories that had been made in this room. As a human, I had died here. Perhaps now it was time to let that girl rest and move on. Though it made my heart ache, I thought that it would probably be a very long time before I came to Ravenworth again.

CHAPTER 12

Luck was on our side and there was a Blood Cross ship in port when we arrived back in London. The *Wraith* was a long, low brig-rigged iron steamer. She was painted gray and carried fourteen guns. The guns made her a little heavy for blockade running, but I felt much safer for having them. The captain agreed to meet with us in our hotel but when he heard where we wanted to go, he staunchly refused. It took the rest of the night and part of the next morning (and several bottles of my whisky) for Devlin and Michael to persuade him otherwise. Finally, he agreed that for the profit he could make running supplies into Savannah it would be worth the small detour on his way to Jamaica.

The only point the men could not get Captain Hines to budge on was the return trip. He would take us to America but he wouldn't postpone his expected arrival in Jamaica while we concluded our business. Since we would have to find another ship to return us to Inverness, it was decided that Devlin would continue on to Jamaica with the *Wraith*. Rose Island, the headquarters of the Blood Cross fleet, was said to lie near those waters and there should be several Blood Cross ships docked at Port Royal. From there Devlin would find another vessel to take us out of America.

Captain Hines insisted on departing the next morning, which meant there were many things to get done in a short amount of time. Devlin, who had seen more wars than he cared to remember in nearly five and a half centuries on this earth, had a list of items we would need to take with us, including a substantial amount of gold.

"You never knew where you're going to get stuck," he said, "and for how long. Guns and gold are the only currency worth carrying in times of war."

That posed a bit of a problem in itself. The guns were easy enough to come by, but getting money out of the Bank of England during business hours is a lot harder than it sounds if you're a vampire. Though we can move about during the day, we have to stay out of direct sunlight or we'll burn. Since I had no wish for my husband to go up in a pillar of fire, this required some planning. Captain Hines loaned us a few men but the excursion required a closed carriage, the largest umbrella I've ever seen, and the cooperation of a darkly overcast winter's day.

With Michael and Devlin taking care of the details

of our voyage, I had little to occupy my time until we set sail the following morning. I spent the afternoon thinking of Fiona, and of all the friends I had loved and lost. When darkness fell, I asked Justine for her company and hailed a carriage. There was one more thing I needed to do before we left England.

We stopped on Panton Street and while Justine paid the driver I stood on the sidewalk, looking up at the sign over the small apothecary shop. *Pendergrass & Company*, it still read. Even though it was well after closing, the lights were on and there was a man at the counter mixing something with a mortar and pestle.

He was tall, with dark hair, and he looked very much like the young apprentice who had often given me candies when I was a child. I smiled, remembering how handsome Archie had seemed to me then, and how he'd won the heart of a ten-year-old girl with a few peppermints. My mother had enjoyed old Mr. Pendergrass's company when we visited London and I had spent many long hours in this shop. Even after Mama's death—especially then—those two men had been my friends. If it hadn't been for Archie and Mr. Pendergrass, I might truly be lying in that grave at Ravenworth.

This young man had to be Archie's son. In profile he had what might have once been Archie's nose, before it had been broken several times during his misspent youth. Had Mr. Pendergrass not taken Archie in and given him an apprenticeship, there's no telling where he might have ended up. I doubted that it would have been with a loving wife, a house full of children, and a thriving business to pass on to his son.

I knocked on the door but, without even looking up, the man at the counter pointed to the closed sign hanging in the window. Not wishing to stand in the street all night, I placed my hand on the door lock and pushed a bit of magic into it, willing it to unlock. There was a soft click and I opened the door. The little bell rang and the man finally looked up. Yes, he did look quite a bit like Archie, though he was a much handsomer, more refined version of his father.

"I'm sorry," he said as Justine and I strolled into the shop. "We're closed."

"What is your name, boy?" Justine asked.

I would have gone with somewhat of a less blunt approach, but that wasn't Justine's way. The poor man looked shocked and mildly offended to be called a boy by a woman who appeared to be no older than twenty-five, but he answered anyway.

"My name is John Little and this is my establishment. And it is closed. Come back tomorrow."

"John," I said calmly. "My name is Cin Craven. This is Justine. We're here to see your father."

He stood silently, looking from me to Justine and back again. I waited patiently for him to realize who we were. I knew he'd figured it out the moment the mortar and pestle hit the floor.

"My God," he whispered. "You're them! Father used to tell me stories of vampires and demons, just as he now tells them to my son. He made all of you sound so very real, but I never actually believed you existed."

"So Archie is still alive?" I asked. "We're not too late?"

A shadow passed over John's face. "Father is bedridden now. He has a cancer."

I closed my eyes for a moment. I'd known that if he was still alive he would be a very old man now. I had tried to prepare myself for anything, but the news that Archie was dying was still hard to take.

"He's in so much pain," John said. "And I'm a coward. Every night he begs me to end his suffering, and every night I come down here and mix the poison he asks for, but I can't bring myself to give it to him."

Archie had been so kind, so selfless. He had done whatever I needed him to do, without question. I hated to think of him as an old man, wasting away in his bed. For a moment I wished I'd never come here. But he'd been a good friend to me, to all of us, and letting him leave this world without saying goodbye—just because it might be easier for me—was wrong.

"May we see him?" I asked softly.

"Of course," John replied, taking a lamp off the table to light our way. "Follow me."

We walked through the private parlor at the rear of the shop, the place where Mr. Pendergrass had sold anything a witch might desire. I was glad to see that Archie had kept it well stocked after Mr. Pendergrass's death. Following John and Justine up the stairs, I glanced back once more at the room where I had spent so much time listening to my mother and Mr. Pendergrass talk of magic.

"Please, come in," John said, and motioned us into the upstairs hall.

Justine and I both knew the apartment above the shop well. Without being told, Justine turned right at the top of the stairs. I started to follow her, but a movement in the dark hallway caught my eye. I turned sharply and the bright lamp John held momentarily destroyed my keen night vision. I motioned John forward and, with the light away from my eyes, I could see an open door down the hall and a young boy peeking out. I smiled and nodded to him and his eyes widened with curiosity. *Archie's grandson by the look of him*, I thought.

Turning, I followed John and Justine into Archie's room. It was here that they'd brought me when I was turned. I'd woken as a vampire in this very room. Oddly, it seemed unsurprising that death still lingered here. And linger it did.

Archie lay, pale and still, in his bed. Several thick blankets were pulled up over his flannel nightshirt to keep him warm. His hair, once black as soot, was now starkly white against his wrinkled, sickly gray skin. What shocked me the most was how small he seemed.

Years ago he'd had a stocky pugilist's frame. Though you couldn't fault the genteel manners Mr. Pendergrass had taught him, Archie had never looked like an apothecary. He'd always looked like what he'd started out as—a street tough who was ready and willing to use his fists, if necessary. Now he was thin and emaciated, a ghost of the man he once was.

I made use of the small chair next to the bed while Justine gently sat down on the mattress, next to Archie's hip. Tenderly, I took his frail hand between both of mine. His eyes fluttered open and he looked at us both for a long time, as if he wasn't sure we were truly there.

"I thought I'd die without ever seeing you again," he said finally.

"It wasn't that I didn't want to come, Archie," I said. "You had a wife and children to provide for, and there are too many vampires in London. It wouldn't have been safe for me to draw attention to you. Besides, I swore to myself that if we made it through that business with Kali, I would leave you and Mr. Pendergrass in peace."

He smiled, though his dark eyes were filled with pain. "Ah, we were fearless, were we not?" he asked.

I chuckled. "I don't know about you two, but I was scared witless through the whole thing."

"Aye, well, perhaps that's true. Time has a way of whitewashing our memories. But *mademoiselle*," he said to Justine, "you are every bit as beautiful as I remember."

Much to Devlin's annoyance, Archie had always been just a little in love with Justine.

"And you are every bit as gallant, my friend," she replied graciously.

He tried to laugh but it came out as racking coughs instead. There was nothing I could do but watch helplessly until he'd once again caught his breath. Archie looked at John, who was standing at the foot of the bed.

"Have you brought it, Johnny?" he asked weakly. Glancing at Justine and me, he added, "I am truly ready to go now. It's time."

John stared at his father, a tear running down his cheek. Without a word he turned and strode from the room.

"Archie," I said softly. "It's a hard thing you ask of him."

Archie closed his eyes. "I know. He's a good son."

He was quiet for a few moments and I thought he had drifted off to sleep. I was about to tuck his hand under the covers and let him rest, when he suddenly squeezed my fingers with a strength I hadn't thought he possessed. My gaze flew to his dark eyes, watching me intently.

"Would you do it for me?" he asked.

"Kill you?"

"Cin, between old age and this disease I hardly remember a time when I wasn't in pain. Please," he begged. "Please make it stop."

I sat there, trying furiously to think of a good reason for denying his request, but I couldn't. It was obvious he was in excruciating pain and his own son would have given him the poison, if he'd been able to bring himself to do it. No child should have to make that choice. But I could. I owed Archie that.

Finally, I said, "Tell me what to mix for the poison and I'll do it."

"Cin!" Justine snapped at me, but I silenced her with a wave of my hand.

"No," Archie said weakly. "Not the poison. Kill me as a vampire would."

"Archie, even in your weakened condition, I couldn't drink enough from you in one feeding to kill you," I explained.

He glanced at Justine. "You could if you both did it."

"*Non*, I will not be a party to this," Justine hissed.

I ignored her. "It might be enough. But I can't guarantee it, Archie."

He closed his eyes. "In all my life I've never felt more alive than I did that one time I fed you, Justine. I would like to feel that once more, before I die."

I glanced at Justine, who was looking tenderly down at Archie. But when she turned her eyes to me they were as hard as blue diamonds. I stood and grabbed her hand.

"Give us a few moments," I said to Archie, and pulled her from the room.

CHAPTER 13

"You cannot be serious," she said as I closed the bed-room door.

"Serious about what?" John asked, confused.

"She wants us to kill your father," Justine snapped.

I sighed. "John, why don't you go in and talk to him. I need to speak with Justine alone."

John looked slightly confused and more than a little alarmed, but he did as I asked. And the minute the door closed behind him Justine started her tirade again.

"It's forbidden to kill humans," she said. "You know that. We execute the monsters who do such things, who break our laws. Or have you forgotten?"

I winced at the comment. Justine and I were as close as sisters, but there had been several times since I became a vampire that she'd looked at me as though I were a monster. But, as Michael always reminded me, we had all made it through those times alive because of the things I'd done. I considered pointing that out to her, but I let it pass.

"I've not forgotten," I said calmly. "I've also not forgotten that it was you who said that mercy was the quality that separated us from the monsters. Is that not what this is, Justine? Mercy?"

She opened her mouth but, having no good answer, snapped it shut again and glared at me.

"Justine, you are the Devil's Justice. I know no one else who has the compassion and empathy that you have. Where are those qualities now? We're not talking about murdering some innocent human. We're talking about ending the suffering of a friend. Don't forget that he freely gave you his blood when you were injured."

She looked away, unable to meet my gaze. "I have not forgotten."

"Archie did whatever we needed him to do, to the point of putting his own life in jeopardy, and he never asked anything of us in return. Justine, he's asking now."

She was quiet for a moment, then she sighed heavily and turned back to me. "I will take his blood," she said. "But I cannot take his life. If you must do this thing, Cin, you will have to drink last."

I nodded. "I wouldn't have asked you to do it any other way."

"Do you bear the burden of his death so easily?" she asked, confused.

I shook my head. Sometimes I wondered if Justine and I would ever understand each other. I had seen her execute hundreds of rogue vampires over the years, and enjoy it. She did her job with a bloodless precision that I would never have, yet she balked at this. I wondered if it was because Archie was human, or because there was no fight in it.

"No," I said finally. "I have many deaths on my conscience, Justine, and I bear none of them lightly. But this is the right thing to do."

Justine and I stood uncomfortably in the hall while Archie said his goodbyes to his son and grandson, Warren. John took the boy back to bed and though I offered for him to return and be with his father in his last moments, he declined.

"We've said everything we wanted to say," he assured me.

"I understand," I replied. "I can promise you that it will be painless, and we'll even make every effort to see that he finds joy in his last moments, but what we're about to do is the stuff of most humans' nightmares. I don't want you to ever wonder if we . . . hurt him in any way. If you want to stay, you're welcome to do so."

"Over the last few months I've often heard him call my mother's name in his delirium, but sometimes," John said, looking over my shoulder at Justine, "he would call hers. Not many seventy-six-year-old men get to die in the

arms of two beautiful women. I'll let him have that moment to himself."

I watched John walk down the hall to his son's room
and then I turned back to Justine.

"When this is over," she said coldly, "I do not ever
want to speak of it again."

I nodded in agreement and followed her into Archie's
room. Justine walked to the far side of the bed and we
sat across from each other, Archie's frail body between
us. There were deep lines between his brows and around
his mouth, but when he saw us he tried to smile through
the pain.

"My girls," he said with a small nod of his head. "I'm
ready."

Justine leaned over him, her face inches from his.
Her hand came up and she stroked the side of his face.
"*Mon cher,*" she said softly, "You remember how this is
done, *non?*"

He looked up at her. "I remember," he said.

His eyes took on a glazed look the moment she bespelled him. I waited for her to drink, but she didn't
move. Just as I was about to open my mouth to speak,
she bent her head to his neck and drank from him more
gently than I'd ever seen her drink from another human.
And he smiled as she did so. When she could take no
more, she pulled back.

Archie took a shuddering breath and opened his eyes.
"So . . . beautiful," he murmured haltingly. Already he

was weaker than I expected. "I . . . would hear . . . you sing . . . once more . . . before I go."

Justine swallowed hard and there was a sadness in her eyes that I had rarely seen. She walked to the foot of the bed and stood there with her back to us for several moments. I gave her the time she needed to compose herself.

"Archie," I said. "Look at me now."

Reluctantly he pulled his eyes from Justine and allowed me to bespell him. When I had him under my control, I glanced back at Justine and nodded. Her gaze flicked quickly from my eyes to Archie's face.

"Look at her," I said. "And listen."

Chills ran through me as Justine's soprano echoed through the room. It was Gounod's *Ave Maria*. Archie's dark eyes stared at her, transfixed, and I wasn't entirely sure whether it was because of vampire magic or the sheer perfection of her voice.

"Goodbye, my friend," I whispered.

I drank deeply—and within minutes Archie Little took his last breath in this world.

CHAPTER 14

Justine stalked into the hotel ahead of me and headed to her room without a word. She was angry with me, but I didn't think it was necessarily because of what we'd done. When you live with someone long enough, you know things without them having to say it. Justine, Devlin, Michael—they all lived in the vampires' world. Since their turning, none of them had cultivated any relationships with humans. Mankind was something to be protected, but merely as a renewable supply of food. And then I'd come along, and I couldn't seem to break free of my ties to humanity. First Fiona's death, and then Archie's . . . they were losses that Justine wouldn't have felt if it hadn't been for me. That's why she was angry.

But she'd been angry with me before, and I with her. It didn't mean we didn't love each other and I knew, once we'd both had time to grieve, things would return to normal. I winced as she slammed the door to her room. When she was upset with Devlin, they fought like wildcats. I envied them that because their arguments raged, but were over quickly. She'd always behaved differently with me, though. It never lasted long, but I would have to endure Justine's silence until she got over her anger. I was never sure who had it easier with her, me or Devlin.

Michael had come out into the hall when Justine slammed her door. "You two have been gone quite a long time," he said. "What's wrong with her?"

"Archie died tonight," I said simply as I walked into our room. I tossed my hat on the bed and just stood there, unsure of what to do now.

"Do you want to talk about it?" he asked.

"No," I replied. "Yes. I held his hand while he died, Michael, and I feel . . . cheated somehow that I wasn't there to do the same with Fiona. I didn't get to say goodbye."

"Sure you did, lass. You said goodbye the last time we left Ravenworth."

"That's not what I meant," I grumbled.

"I know it's not," Michael said softly. "But you've known for many years now that every time you say farewell, it may be the last time. Right now you wish you'd been there, but Fiona would not have wanted that and I think, deep down, you wouldn't either."

"Perhaps not," I admitted. "But I should have been there for her, as I was with Archie. Of the two of them, it should have been her I was with in those final moments."

Michael was silent for a moment. "Close your eyes," he said, "and think of Archie. Tell me what you see."

I did as he asked and I saw a sick old man.

"You don't remember the big, handsome young man who helped us fight a demon, do you?"

I wiped a tear from the corner of my eye. "No," I replied.

"But when you think of Fi she's always young, strong, and beautiful, is she not? It's the way she'd want to be remembered by you, not as an old woman on her deathbed. She wouldn't want you to see that every time you thought of her."

I looked up at him. "What would I do without you?"

"Ah, lass. You expect too much of yourself. The world wouldn't come crashing to a halt if you were a little selfish every now and then, you know."

"Hmmm. I'll have to remember that the next time we're in bed."

"See that you do, *mo ghraidh*, and I will happily service you in whatever way you demand," he teased. "But right now we have a ship to board and a damsel in distress to rescue."

Yes, the ship would sail with the morning tide and

we had to be on it before sunrise. I was worried for Claire and her family, but a small part of me was glad to have something else to focus on besides the pain of death. For possibly the first time in my life, I was happy to leave England behind.

CHAPTER 15

The voyage across the Atlantic only took a couple of weeks, during which time we all repeatedly thanked our respective gods for the invention of the steam engine. Devlin had never been a good sailor and to say that he was miserable was an understatement. It's funny how I often forget how very large and intimidating he is until he's cranky. This had not escaped the notice of the human sailors, though, and they all tried valiantly to stay out of his way. For the most part Devlin remained in his cabin, where I assumed Justine did her best to keep him occupied. That was fine with me. The tension between us had eased somewhat, but she was still often terse and moody in my company.

We made port at St. George in Bermuda for a few days to take on some supplies and allow Devlin to walk on dry land again. Mostly, though, Captain Hines simply wanted to wait until the moon was waning before we attempted to sail into Savannah. The Union blockade was sparse and largely ineffectual, but the captain wanted to take as few risks as possible with his ship. It would be much easier to run into Savannah under the cover of a moonless night.

Shortly after full dark on the night of the new moon we all stood on the deck of the *Wraith*, searching the dark waters for any sign of Union gunboats. The crew all breathed a sigh of relief when we sailed into the Savannah River Channel unmolested. I think Michael was a bit disappointed that he didn't get to witness a great chase on the high seas, with cannons firing. In truth, perhaps, I was as well but one look at the way Devlin stood hunched over with his arms braced on the railing and I couldn't imagine how he would have survived it. Seasickness won't kill a vampire, of course, but it might make him long for a nice, sharp wooden stake.

Michael offered to go to Jamaica in Devlin's place but that proposal only served to wound our leader's masculine pride. Devlin drew himself up and announced with great indignation (which would have come off much better if he hadn't been a tad green), "I have fought countless horrifically bloody battles in more wars than you will ever see. I think I can manage to make it to Jamaica and back."

And that was the end of that discussion. I felt sorry for Devlin, and responsible for his discomfort. He'd made this journey for me, after all, to help a member of my family. I pulled Michael aside as the sailors were bringing our trunks up from our cabins.

"I want you to ask Justine to stay with Devlin," I told him.

"Not that I have an objection," Michael said, "but why?"

"Because Devlin will be happier with that arrangement, and so will she. And you might suggest that they take a few days to rest before they return. We'll be fine here and I hate to put Devlin through a return trip immediately. Also," I added, "I think perhaps some time apart would be good for Justine and me."

Michael put his arms around me. "I believe she's been thinking of her sister," he said softly. "And I think she's a little jealous of you right now."

"Jealous?" I said, incredulously.

"You know that she made the decision to cut all ties to her human life when she disappeared from the stage of the Paris Opera—and from her life in the king's court—to become a vampire. Though she and Devlin stayed in Paris until Solange died, she never spoke to her sister again. You and Fiona had the sort of relationship that Justine and Solange never had, and you continued that relationship even after you were turned. I think maybe Justine is envious of that. It's not your fault, but you must let her work through it in her own head."

"I know," I said. "It just makes me sad."

"What makes you sad?" Devlin asked, coming up behind us. "If you tell me it's getting off this damned ship, I just might throttle you."

I laughed and cast a pointed look at Michael. He took the opportunity to nod meaningfully to Justine and the two of them hung back to talk as Devlin and I disembarked.

"The captain says we have a few hours in port while he offloads his cargo," I observed as we left the ship. "What would you like to do?"

"Have a proper meal, for one thing. I'm starving," he said, and wobbled a bit on his feet as we stepped onto the gangplank.

I took his arm, as I would take the arm of any gentleman, but my intention at the moment was simply to steady him. I glanced up at him, but his face held that determined look I'd come to know so well. He was more convinced than I was that he could walk without falling over. As I was certain he would find it offensive if I asked him if he needed a moment, I dropped my reticule instead. Kneeling down, I intentionally picked it up from the bottom, scattering its contents across the wooden planks. Michael and Justine caught up to us and the three of us retrieved my belongings while Devlin stood perfectly still and allowed his body to become accustomed to ground that didn't move under his feet. As Justine handed me several coins and a handkerchief, I winked at her. She smiled—the first genuine smile I'd seen from her in weeks—and stifled a laugh. By the time we were ready to continue on our way, Devlin looked much more capable of walking under his own power. And they say women are vain.

We took a carriage into Savannah, carrying with us only the trunk filled with gold. Sailors from the *Wraith* would deliver the rest of our belongings to the Pulaski House hotel, which the old man driving the carriage had assured us was one of the grandest hotels in town, after their cargo had been offloaded. As we drove along the wide thoroughfares, we questioned our driver about the city and the various districts we passed through. It was always nice to know where the best hunting might be found.

Savannah was as lovely a city as I had ever seen. Unlike London at this time of year, the gardens and town squares were filled with green leaves and blooming flowers. I quickly fell in love with the brightly colored azaleas, the abundant hydrangeas, the exotic palms, and the oak trees dripping with Spanish moss. I could have happily enjoyed the scenery for hours, but shortly the carriage pulled to a stop in front of the Pulaski House. Justine and I strolled into the hotel's spacious lobby, glancing around appreciatively at the marble interior. The men followed behind us with the trunk, waving off the two black porters who rushed up to relieve them of their burden. It was incredibly heavy and I knew they didn't want anyone speculating as to what was inside.

"I require a room, please," I said to the man standing behind the highly polished front desk.

He was short, with a round, ruddy face and a receding hairline. Spectacles perched gingerly on his bulbous nose, making his whole face appear more jovial than I was used to seeing from clerks in fine hotels. They were usually a starchy, pompous lot. It made me smile at him and he flushed, his clear blue eyes shifting from me to Justine and then to the men.

"One room or two?" he asked.

"My husband and I are the only ones who will be staying," I replied. "And since we do have rather a lot of baggage to be delivered from the docks I would like the largest suite you have available."

"Certainly, ma'am," he said, taking note of my accent and my expensive clothes, of the large ruby wedding ring on my finer and the ruby and diamond cross hanging around my neck. I wondered how much he was mentally raising the price of our room. I wouldn't quibble, though. I had a feeling they would need whatever money they could get in the years to come.

"Is there a bank nearby, sir?" Michael inquired.

The clerk nodded. "The Merchants and Planters Bank is just down the street."

I smiled at him again, just to see if I could make his cheeks turn that charming shade of pink once more. After that it didn't take any sort of vampire magic to gain his full cooperation. "If you would be so kind, would you have a messenger request that the manager of that fine establishment meet with my husband in our room tomorrow afternoon?"

"I would be more than happy to assist you with that," he assured me. Thankfully he was so flustered he didn't inquire as to why I couldn't simply walk down the street to the bank myself. Or perhaps he assumed I was a titled English lady who was used to having the world at my beck and call. Whatever the case, he was eager to please.

"If you require anything else," he insisted, "my name is Mr. Bennett."

Michael signed the guest book and took the key from Mr. Bennett. The helpful clerk asked if we'd like the porters to assist us in carrying the trunk to our room, but Michael and Devlin again declined the offer. We quickly found our suite on the second floor and the men deposited the heavy trunk at the foot of the bed.

Michael glanced at the clock. "It shouldn't take long to unload the ship," he said. "And Captain Hines has made it abundantly clear that he doesn't want to linger in port. We should eat and then return to the docks as soon as possible."

"I don't understand why the captain won't wait one more night," I said, frustrated. "Tomorrow night we'll go out to this island, get Claire, and be done with it."

"Because," Devlin replied, "by tomorrow morning every Union ironclad patrolling these waters will know that a ship slipped past them tonight, and Hines won't take the risk that they'll be waiting at the mouth of the river for him to come out again."

"Devlin's right," Michael agreed. "We have a better chance of getting out of here if they go tonight and come back for us."

I reluctantly agreed and hoped they were right.

CHAPTER 16

Before we left the hotel, I laid a keep-away spell on the door. Designed to give humans a sense of dread and unease, I used it to deter would-be thieves. It was a small spell I'd learned from Aunt Maggie decades ago after my jewelry had been stolen from our hotel in Inverness, and one of the only bits of spellcraft I actually practiced.

Since time was of the essence, the first order of business was to find a hot meal. The way Devlin and Michael had been complaining of hunger, that would have topped my list even if we hadn't been short on time. One of the benefits of traveling on a Blood Cross ship was that the entire fleet was manned by sailors whose families had worked for the shipping line for decades, if not centuries. Though they willingly took turns feeding us, it was considered bad form to abuse their hospitality by drinking too deeply. Consequently, for the last several weeks we had all drunk just enough to survive. Now that we were free to hunt, our bodies yearned to finally be full and sated.

I glanced down at my dark blue dress with its belled skirt and wished I could change into my breeches and boots. I didn't want to do anything, though, that might attract attention to us in this new city. America wasn't like Europe. It was relatively new territory for vampires and it had no kings, no regents, and no laws. The High King would have to take it under his control soon, but until he did we were not The Righteous here, we were simply a group of unknown vampires trespassing in the city. For all I knew we could be the only vampires in the area. However, since we hadn't come all this way to waste time with territorial squabbles, we tried our best to pass as human. Unfortunately for me, that meant skirts and hoops and crinolines.

"I think we should spilt up," Devlin suggested. "We'll attract less attention if we aren't hunting in a pack."

Michael and I agreed and the two of us began walking east, while Devlin and Justine faded into the night in the opposite direction. We were moving back toward the docks and I recognized many of the buildings. During the ride to the hotel I'd overheard Michael's whispered inquiry to our driver about the location of any brothels in the city. The old man had not commented but he had nodded discreetly in the general direction of the waterfront. Before long Michael and I found ourselves standing in the shadows across the street from one such establishment. We watched as a group of soldiers walked in and several came out.

"What do you think?" Michael asked.

"I think it's either a whorehouse or Confederate headquarters," I said dryly.

Though I hated to watch my husband walk into a brothel, it was expedient. I knew he would pay for an hour of some girl's time, take her blood, and leave her with only a pleasant memory. The bite marks would heal and fade before she saw her next customer.

"I think if you were to go in, and I were to take a walk, we could wrap this up quickly," I observed.

He pulled me close and I looked into his eyes, then down to his sensual, kissable lips.

"Be careful," he said.

"Behave," I replied.

"Always," he murmured, and his lips met mine.

"Go," I said, pulling away before I wanted to. "And we can finish that kiss in bed."

He grinned down at me wickedly, kissed me swiftly, and walked away. I sighed and looked up and down the street. *Now, what dark corner of Savannah do you suppose a girl has to linger in to get assaulted?* I wondered.

There were reasons Michael wasn't loitering with me on the darkened city streets. For one, taking some-one's blood is an intimate act, whether you want it to be or not. That was why Michael and Devlin were so hungry. Onboard ship, the only available blood was from other men and Michael and Devlin's sexual preferences in no way ran toward the same sex. Even though none of us had taken much blood from the sailors, the men had taken even less than Justine and me.

Also, hunting is different for men and women. None of us has a taste for taking the blood of innocent humans. When I bit someone, it was usually because he deserved it. Justine and I often hunted together, finding that there's a never-ending supply of criminals in the less savory districts of any city. For the men, though, it was not so easy. You rarely found a female out at night, committing nefarious deeds. So I didn't begrudge Michael his whores. I would much rather he drink from a woman who made her living selling her body, than from a mother hurrying home to her family after a hard day's work in some factory.

Normally the hunting would be plentiful for both of us after a long sea voyage, but now I found that our situations were reversed. In Savannah, a good portion of the population's males were either enlisted in the city's militia or off at war. Since I refused to consider any male in uniform as prey, I began to wonder if I would end up having to feed from someone I normally wouldn't. Fortunately for me and my growing hunger, if there was one thing that was true about the human race the world over, it was this: if you're a female out by yourself at night, some man will hassle you. It didn't take long before my next meal found me.

I was wandering down a quiet side street, somewhere near the waterfront. Several soldiers in gray Confederate uniforms passed at the end of the street, and I fell back into the shadows as they went by. They seemed so young, little more than boys fighting a man's war. Before I had time to dwell on that, I heard footsteps coming down the street. I turned and watched the man walk toward me.

He appeared to be a gentleman, at least until he moved closer. The clothes that hung loosely on his thin frame were of a good cut and quality, but it was obvious they had not been made for him. I wondered if they had been given to him as charity, or if he'd stolen them. His graying hair was unkempt, as was the stubble upon his chin and cheeks. In one hand he swung a silver-tipped walking stick. I turned my head and ignored him, giving him the opportunity to pass me by. But he didn't.

"My, my," he drawled. "Would you lookit all that red hair. Sure wouldn't mind a taste of cherry pie tonight."

I arched a brow at him. "I am not a whore, sir. I'm merely waiting for my husband. Good evening to you," I said sharply.

He moved even closer to me. "Fancy cherries, at that. Now, ain't that interesting? I hear you English girls are as frigid as a Yankee winter but I reckon you'd be a hot piece, wouldn't you? You know what they say, red on the head, fire in the—"

"Sir!" I exclaimed, feigning shocked indignation. "You company is not welcome."

I turned to walk away, unhappy with my close proximity to the busier road at the end of the block. I should have stayed farther down the street where it was less likely someone would see me drinking. Hopefully, this obnoxious man would follow. I'd barely taken a step when the end of his walking stick slammed into the brick wall, mere inches away from my face.

"Little bit of a thing like you shouldn't be out by yourself at night," he whispered in my ear. "Lawless times like these, some man's liable to take it into his head to do no tellin' what to that pretty body." I stood perfectly still as he leaned farther into me, bracing his hand on the wall behind my head, trapping me on all sides. "And if you didn't please him just right, well, he might even take it into his head to kill you."

He was so aroused I could almost feel the blood hammering through his veins. My canines lengthened and sharpened in response and I turned my head, smiling as his eyes widened in fear.

"Then it's a good thing I'm already dead," I replied before I snatched the walking stick out of his hand, jerked his head back, and sank my teeth into his neck.

CHAPTER 17

"How long have you lived in Savannah?" I asked as I wiped the blood from my lips.

The man huddled on the ground, sobbing. He'd been so repulsive that I hadn't bothered to bespell him before I drank. I'd wager his neck hurt like hell right about now. Disgusted, I sank down before him, my skirts making a soft whoosh that caused him to look up.

"Stop sniveling," I said and locked my gaze with his. When he was in thrall, I repeated my question.

"Lived here all my life," he answered readily.

"Good," I said. "I have some questions and you will answer them fully and honestly, do you understand?"

He nodded. "Yes, ma'am."

"Do you know of a man named Adrien Boucher?" I asked.

"Yes."

"I want you to tell me everything you know about him."

"Damned uppity Cajun is what he is," he replied, with more candor than I had expected. "Came here about fifteen years ago from Louisiana. Said his father owned a big plantation down by New Orleans, but I never believed it. He sure managed to charm the skirts right off Miss Evangeline Peyton, though. Tongue like a viper, that girl, but damned if she wasn't the prettiest thing in Savannah or the islands. I don't know what she ever saw in Adrien Boucher but he married her just as quick as he could get her to the altar."

"Boucher is married?" I asked, surprised. I wondered what his wife had to say about him bringing Claire back from England with him.

The man shrugged. "Ain't no one seen her in years. She's rarely left that island since her daddy died. Old man Peyton had all the money, see, and that's all Boucher was after. Miss Evangeline, she came and went as she pleased while her daddy was alive but as soon as the old man dropped dead, her trips into Savannah became few and far between. Personally, I think Boucher's killed her."

I frowned. "Why would you think that?"

"Because her daddy never trusted banks," he stated firmly, as if that explained it all. I must have looked confused because he began to elaborate. "Hell, old Peyton never trusted anybody. They say that in his youth he was run out of England on a rail for being part of some-thing called a hellfire club."

Interesting, I thought. There had been a number of so-called hellfire clubs in England over the years, some more notorious than others. They were secret gentle-men's clubs formed by the aristocracy's most profligate rakes and scoundrels. Their activities were said to range widely from common pranks on the local populace to wild orgies or even devil worship.

Obviously such rumors had followed Peyton to America because the man added, "Don't know what manner of perversions he was practicing, but it must have been something awful 'cause his family's title and money couldn't protect him. So he came here, bought Devil's Island and a whole passel of slaves, and built himself a fine plantation."

I shook my head. "What does that have to do with banks, or why you think Boucher has murdered his wife?"

He leaned forward and said in a conspiratorial whis-per, "Because whatever money he used to do all that, no bank in Savannah's ever seen. They say he's got chests of gold buried out on that island. Maybe Miss Evan-geline told Boucher where they was buried and now he don't need her anymore. Or maybe he asked and she refused to say. A man might kill a woman for that. All I know is that Boucher comes and goes, but ain't no one laid eyes on Miss Evangeline in over two years."

"Interesting," I murmured. "And if I wanted to go to this Devil's Island, how would I get there?"

"There's only one dock on Devil's Island. If you try to fetch up anywhere else, you gonna have to trek through forests or salt marshes. Last man to go out there uninvited came back with an ass full of buckshot. I don't know anyone who'd be crazy enough to take you out there, except maybe Ben Hennessey. But he won't do it for money."

"What will he do it for?" I asked.

"White lightning," he replied.

I stared at him blankly. "I don't know what that means."

"Moonshine," he elaborated. I shook my head again. "Corn whiskey, ma'am!"

Ah, whisky was something I understood. "I have Scotch whisky," I offered.

"A bottle of that should buy a boat ride to Devil's Island. But Hennessey only likes the cheap stuff."

I narrowed my eyes. "I don't have any *cheap stuff*."

He shrugged. "I guess it'll do, then, what with the shortage of liquor these days."

Oh, the thoughts of one of my lovely bottles of fifteen-year-old Glenlivet in the hands of a—I gritted my teeth. If that's what it took to get to Claire, then it was a small price to pay. I stood and looked down at the man, realizing I'd never even asked his name. Not that it mattered.

I had what I came for and there was only one thing left to do.

"Look at me," I said and his eyes snapped up to mine. "You won't remember any of this. The last thing you'll be able to recall is turning onto this street. And you won't ever behave to another woman the way you did to me tonight, will you?" I asked, my voice harsh with implied violence.

"No, ma'am," he quickly assured me. "I can damned sure guarantee you that."

Because I'd drunk from him, he would be compelled to obey any direct order from me. It was one of the powers that vampires acquire shortly after their turning, along with the ability to bespell a human and the rapid healing rate of a bite wound. If I didn't feed from him regularly, though, my control would fade in a few days. Then again, who really knew what lingered in the shadowy depths of our minds? Perhaps that voice that lives inside us all—the one that reminds us that there are things in the dark that will hurt us—would keep him from harming another woman. Perhaps not. But it was the best I could do.

CHAPTER 18

I lay on the bed on my stomach, once again studying the map we'd purchased of Savannah and its islands before Devlin and Justine had left on the *Wraith*. Devil's Island was easy to find, exactly where Raina's location spell had said it would be, but it was difficult to determine how long it would take to get there. I had no idea what sort of boat this man Hennessey owned. If it wasn't steam powered we'd never make it that far down the coast and back to Savannah by dawn. Not for the first time, I cursed the fact that I could no longer walk in the sun as a human. It was going to look a trifle odd, us showing up on someone's private island in the middle of the night. Then again, the bastard had kidnapped my cousin. If that didn't warrant two vampires knocking on your door in the dead of night, I didn't know what did.

Michael got out of bed and crossed the room to retrieve a bottle of whisky from the dressing table. I glanced up, admiring the sleek, powerful lines of his naked body. The only thing that marred the view was those horrid curtains. Since hotels often frown on their patrons boarding up the windows or painting over them, one of the essentials we always travelled with were several sets of thick, black canvas curtains. There were not the least bit aesthetically pleasing, but they did a marvelous job of keeping out the sun.

Michael returned to bed with the whisky, taking a long draw and then offering me the bottle. I took a sip, handed it back to him, and returned to studying my map. I felt the mattress dip under his weight and seconds later cool liquid ran down my spine to pool at the small of my back. I shivered as Michael licked the whisky from my skin, then continued trailing kisses up my back.

"Haven't you had enough?" I asked, laughing.

"I'll never have enough of you," he said hotly as he slid his body against mine and peered over my shoulder. "What are you looking at?"

"Just trying to get my bearings," I replied, tapping the map with one finger. "This is where we're going."

Michael wasn't really paying attention. He'd seen it earlier when I had shared what I'd learned from the man in the alley with him and Devlin and Justine.

"And we're just going to walk in and take Claire, is that it?" Michael asked as he kissed the side of my neck.

I looked back over my shoulder at him. "How is Boucher going to stop us?"

"Indeed," he replied. "Then all we have to do is keep her safe until Devlin and Justine return from Jamaica. That might not be as easy as it sounds, love."

"Yes, I was thinking about that. Perhaps we should rent a house. It'll take them at least two weeks to get back to Savannah and I think a house would be a much better defensive position, just in case Boucher tries to take her back."

"It's a good idea," Michael agreed. "Since Mr. Bennett was so helpful in getting that greedy man from the bank to come by this morning, perhaps you should ask him to send us an estate agent tomorrow?"

I smiled briefly, thinking of the look on the banker's face when Michael had dropped a bag of gold coins in his lap. "Yes," I said dreamily, "Mr. Bennett is ever so helpful."

Michael laughed and returned to trailing kisses up my shoulder to my neck. "As long as he isn't *too* helpful."

I glanced over my shoulder at my husband. "Jealous?" I teased.

"Not in the slightest," he murmured as he settled himself between my legs.

I sighed happily. "By the gods, you are insatiable."

He gently bit the back of my neck. "Only when it comes to you, *mo ghraidh*."

Ben Hennessey was some sort of fisherman. At least that's the way it appeared from the nets piled in his boat and the pungent aroma of fish and saltwater that emanated from his person. By the looks of his derelict boat he couldn't be too successful at his trade, or perhaps he simply drank up all his profits. He was a big man with blond hair and bushy sideburns. It was difficult to tell his age because the sun and the liquor had taken their toll; he could have been thirty or fifty, or anywhere in between. He shuffled across the deck of his small steam-powered fishing vessel with a painful-looking gait. There was something wrong with his right leg, which was probably why he was plying his trade here instead of fighting in the war.

"Mr. Hennessey," Michael called from the dock. "I have a job for you."

Hennessey tipped his hat back and looked up at us. "I reckon I already got a job, mister."

Michael held up the bottle of whisky. "One trip down the coast to Devil's Island in exchange for a bottle of fifteen-year-old Glenlivet single malt."

Hennessey eyed the bottle covetously. "Well, now, why didn't you say so in the first place? Although, Devil's Island—" he said with a lick of his lips and a remorseful shaking of his head. "Take a chance on gettin' shot goin' there. Seems to me a man's life is surely worth two bottles of whisky, don't you think?"

"Oh, for the love of Danu," I muttered.

"Done!" Michael agreed, and hopped down into the boat. The little craft was so shoddy that I had momentary visions of him going right through the floor. He handed Hennessey the bottle with the promise of the second one upon our safe return. Then he turned and grasped me by the waist and swung me into the boat.

"You're wantin' to go now?" Hennessey asked. "In the dark?"

"Is that a problem?" I inquired.

"No," he said, shaking his head thoughtfully. "No, ma'am, I guess it ain't."

Hennessey fired up the engine while Michael untied the craft from its mooring. The boat had a shallow draft and we hugged the coastline as close as we could to avoid running afoul of any Union gunboats. The trip was interminably long and made worse by the fact that the night was warm and the fog had rolled in. As a result, my lovely green dress was damp and my coiffure was probably ruined. For the first time I was grateful for the popularity of hoop skirts. If it hadn't been for the belled foundation garment, my skirt would undoubtedly have been clinging obscenely to my legs.

"There she is," Hennessey said gravely. "Devil's Island."

There were no lights, nor anything that indicated this stretch of land was any different than the miles of shadowy shoreline we'd already passed. I trusted that Hennessey knew these waters, though, and watched expectantly as he piloted the boat into an inlet between the island and the mainland. The night was eerily quiet, which seemed to magnify the sound of the steam engine. I was certain that anyone for miles around could hear us coming. Perhaps that's why I wasn't surprised to see a lone figure on the dock ahead of us. As we got closer I could tell that it was a woman. She was standing still as a statue, holding a lantern aloft. It was as if she'd been waiting for us.

"Anyone but me find that peculiar?" Hennessey mumbled.

I glanced at Michael, but he just shrugged. As Hennessey steered the boat to the dock and Michael tied it up, my eyes were riveted to the woman. The light illuminated her face, casting shadows under her high cheekbones and a golden hue to her cocoa skin. She was dressed entirely in white, from the turban covering her hair to the blouse and skirt she wore. She was young, perhaps in her late twenties, but her dark eyes held wisdom beyond her years. She stared at me, never once looking at Michael or Mr. Hennessey, and I found it hard to drag my gaze from hers.

I heard Michael turn to Hennessey and whisper, "If you're not here when we get back, you won't live long enough to finish that bottle."

Michael leapt onto the dock and I looked up at him as he reached down and helped me from the boat. It was unnecessary, but it was a polite gesture. As soon as my feet hit the boards, though, I turned back to the woman. This close to her, I could feel it. She had magic.

"I been waitin' for you," she said to me, her voice thick with a lilting accent I hadn't heard in Savannah. "I told him you would come. You won't be gettin' the girl, but I expect you'll be wantin' to see that for yourself. Come."

She turned and strode off, carrying herself like a queen. With no other option before us, Michael and I followed her. A long, wide road led from the dock, running straight into the center of the island. Giant oaks rose up on either side of the road, their branches forming a canopy over our heads. There must have been hundreds of them stretching out into the distance. Up ahead, perhaps a half mile down the tree-lined drive, I could see the lights of a great house.

"What's your name?" I asked the woman, thinking that it was going to be a long, quiet walk and perhaps she could be induced to tell me something useful.

"I am Pandora," she replied.

"Do you work in Mr. Boucher's house?" Michael inquired.

She laughed. "I do many things for the master."

I inwardly cringed at her use of the word "master." The practice of slavery was repellent to me and I wondered with distaste exactly what sort of things Boucher forced her to do for him. By the color of her skin it was obvious that there were least one or two white men in Pandora's ancestry, and I could think of little that was worse than being owned by a man that you had no right to say no to. Whether or not Boucher was like these men,

Pandora still called him master and that made me want to bite him all the more.

Such thoughts flitted in and out of my head as we walked quietly to the house. Pandora's terse answers discouraged any more questions, so I simply held Michael's hand and enjoyed the majesty of the oaks and the songs of the night birds in the trees. I wanted to find the whole island as distasteful as I found Boucher but, in truth, I wasn't sure I'd ever seen anything more beautiful. Before long, the tunnel-like corridor of the drive opened up and gave way to an expansive lawn leading up to the plantation house.

"Welcome to Kenneway," Pandora proudly announced.

It was exactly the way I'd envisioned a southern plantation house would look, sitting like a dazzling white pearl against the green velvet lawn. Eight Doric columns marched in stately elegance along the front of the house, supporting two stories of wide porches with finely wrought iron railings. Many such railings and decorative iron-works in Savannah had been removed and melted down to help the war effort. Kenneway's iron still stood, though, like delicate black lace, perfectly complementing the black shutters that graced each of the eight tall windows. As if on cue, the double front doors swung open and I came face to face with Adrien Boucher.

I could well imagine what Miss Evangeline Peyton had seen in this man. He was in his mid-to-late forties and he had a sleek, hungry look about him, very sophisticated and urbane. His rich brown hair was slicked back with not a strand out of place and there was something quite temptingly dangerous about his eyes. They were the same golden brown as a tiger's, and his swarthy skin only added to his exotic appeal.

"Don't look into their eyes," Pandora whispered to him as she sailed through the door. "She's a powerful bokor. I can feel her magic crawlin' across my skin like a thousand tiny ants."

Adrien's lips twitched in a smile under his thin mustache but I noticed that he heeded her advice. His eyes focused just below mine, but never met them directly. By doing this he insured that I couldn't use vampire magic to bespell him, and I was hesitant to use my regular magic at this point because of Pandora. She could feel my power, but I could also feel hers. There was darkness in it and I'd learned long ago not to tangle with black magic unless it was absolutely necessary. If we could get into the house, though, brute force would accomplish our goal.

"Mr. Boucher, I believe we have some business to discuss," I said. "May we come in?"

He smiled. "I think not. I believe I am much safer with the threshold between us, Mrs. —?"

I narrowed my eyes and looked at Pandora. She knew what we were and that we couldn't enter the house without an invitation. Somehow she'd known before we'd even arrived.

"My name is Cin Craven and you are in possession of my cousin Claire," I said coldly. "I want her back."

"I would be happy to return the girl to you," Boucher announced, "but she has something I want and until she gives it to me she will not leave this house."

There were several ways to interpret such a statement and I didn't care for any of them. "If you've hurt her in any way—"

Boucher held up one hand. "I've not harmed the girl," he said. "Yet. But I am running out of time and patience. Perhaps you can convince her to do what's right. Mr. McCready!"

The doors off the central hallway opened and a stocky man with a bushy red beard and a halo of carrot-colored curls entered the hall. His beefy hand was wrapped around a young lady's wrist as he dragged her behind him. I knew this was Claire, for she had the stamp of the Macgregors on her—a head full of thick, coppery curls pulled back in a simple bow at the nape of her neck. She was a pretty girl with her father's height and her mother's face. Her celery green dress was a trifle loose and though she looked too thin, I could see no marks or other visible signs of abuse. I expected her to be frightened but her blue eyes were merely cautious, and angry.

"Claire," I said, gaining her attention. "We've never met, but I'm your cousin, Cin Craven. Your mother sent me to bring you home." I held my hand out to her. "Whatever he wants, give it to him and come with me."

Her anger melted away at the mention of Raina and her expression softened. A tear slipped down her cheek. Mr. McCready still held her wrist but he released it when she raised her hand to wipe away the tear. I didn't like the way his small, round eyes watched her covetously.

"Tell my parents I'm sorry, but I can't do it." She looked to Boucher and her eyes hardened. "I *won't* do it," she said mutinously, "and you can't make me!"

With that she picked up her skirts, turned on her heel and, with a toss of her copper curls, marched up the stairs. My mouth fell open as I watched her storm off. I wasn't sure what was going on; this spitfire was certainly was not the fragile, damaged young girl Raina had led me to believe I'd find. When Claire reached the top of the stairs she was met by a tall, lovely brunette in full evening dress. The woman made some comment, but Claire held one hand up dismissively and strode past her.

"Gold," I said, jerking my attention back to Boucher. "I have quite a lot of it. Name your price for her freedom."

"While your offer is tempting, I'm afraid what she possesses is without price," he said as he nonchalantly pulled a pocket watch from his vest. He flipped the lid open and looked down at the time. "You'd be wise to return to your boat, Cin Craven. If you take shelter anywhere on this island, I'll know about it and I will see you burned come the dawn."

And with that he closed the door in our faces.

"What the hell just happened?" I said, more to myself than to Michael.

When he didn't respond, I turned to him. He was leaning back against one of the columns, staring at the front doors with a thoughtful expression on his face. "Why didn't you say anything?" I prodded.

"You seemed to be handling everything as well as could be expected, given that for once the element of surprise was not on our side," he replied. "Besides, I was busy noticing other things."

"What things?" I asked.

He held his hand out to me. "Come on," he said leading me off the porch, "before Mr. Hennessey drinks himself into a stupor."

"But what are we supposed to do now?" I asked.

"We tried it your way," he replied. "Now we're going to go back to Savannah and try it my way."

"Your way usually involves a sword and a lot of fighting," I pointed out.

"Very true, my dear, but I'm getting wiser in my old age," he said smugly.

I narrowed my eyes at the self-satisfied smile on his face. "What are you planning?"

Michael slid his arm around my waist. "Why don't you let me surprise you?"

CHAPTER 19

Mr. Barie from the Merchants and Planters Bank arrived at the Pulaski House bright and early at the ungodly hour of nine o'clock. As I was still in bed (where all vampires should be at nine in the morning), Michael escorted the banker to an adjacent room that Mr. Bennett had allowed him to use for the meeting. I briefly wondered what my husband was up to but, before I could dwell on it much further, sleep claimed me again. Perhaps an hour later I woke as the bed dipped and Michael gently shook my shoulder.

"Cin, I need you to wake up for a moment and sign this," he said.

I rose up off my stomach and pushed my hair out of my face. I signed where I was told and then Michael snatched up the papers, kissed me on the forehead, and rushed off again. By the time he returned I was awake and waiting.

I was used to signing financial documents for him. Rarely did I understand what I was putting my name to, but I did understand account balances. Michael was a genius with money and he handled all the finances for our group. Over the years he'd taken the substantial inheritance I'd received from my father and built a fortune that even a frivolous woman would be unable to spend in many lifetimes. I trusted him implicitly with my money, but he was up to something and I wanted to know what it was.

"What did I sign?" I asked. "And what is going on, Michael?"

He tossed some papers on the bed and then swept me into his arms. "My beautiful wife, I have an early birthday present for you," he said. "You are now the proud owner of Devil's Island and Kenneway Plantation."

My mouth fell open. "What are you talking about? How is that possible?"

"I told you, last night I was busy noticing other things. Like the discolored places on the walls and floors. Paintings and carpets that once graced that mansion have recently been sold."

"And that led you to believe—"

"That Boucher is in need of funds and that it was possible he'd mortgaged Kenneway to a bank in Savannah," Michael explained.

"But what about all that gold?" I asked. "There's supposed to be trunks of it buried on the island."

Michael shrugged. "Maybe Boucher really did kill his wife when she refused to tell him where her father's money was hidden."

I shook my head. "No, she's alive. I saw her at the top of the stairs last night. At least, I assume that was Evangeline. Who else would it be?"

"Then maybe Peyton's gold is just a myth and there was never any to begin with. Or perhaps he spent it all building his plantation. All I know is that just before the war started Boucher mortgaged Kenneway to the hilt. And you, my dear, just bought the mortgage."

I glanced at the papers on the bed. "Can I do that?"

"You can and you did," he replied with a grin.

I smiled back. "What does that mean?"

"That means that we can go back out there tonight and call in the mortgage. If he can't pay it, then you have the right to evict him."

At that my jubilance floundered. "Yes, and getting him out of that house worked so well last night."

"Ah, but now you *own* the house," he said. "We can walk right in the front door."

"That's true, but he's not going to leave willingly. And he has a witch of his own. It's not that I doubt my abilities, it's just that going toe to toe with someone steeped in the dark arts can get rather messy, and rarely ends well."

"Then we'll think of some way to do it safely. After all, we have the rest of the day to make plans," Michael said as he lifted me off my feet and spun me around, depositing me in front of the wardrobe.

I thought that perhaps he meant to have me right up against the doors but the sound of breaking glass fore-stalled any amorous intentions on either of our parts. As did the canvas curtains that swiftly went up in flames. Michael rushed forward, but I grabbed his arm.

"What exactly do you think you're going to do?" I asked frantically.

After all, vampires and fire do not mix. I threw on my dressing gown and opened the door. There was a hotel porter walking down the hall to the stairs, just a few feet away.

"Fire!" I screamed. "Fire!"

The porter spun on his heel and raced back down the hall, pushing me aside as he rushed into the room. The other hotel guests began peering out of their rooms and then quickly exiting the floor when they realized it wasn't a false alarm. Two more porters ran up the steps followed by a man I assumed to be Mr. Bennett's day-time counterpart. Between them they managed to tear down the curtains and began trying to stomp out the flames. When they had it nearly under control I helped them out with a little push of magic.

"Extinguish," I whispered, and the flames died out.

"Why didn't you just do that in the first place?" Michael said softly into my ear as he placed his coat around my shoulders.

I looked up at him. "Well, I would have if I'd accidentally started the blaze, but I do believe someone just tried to kill us. It seemed a good idea to have witnesses. Besides, running from the room and screaming 'fire' is what a human would do."

When the clerk and the porters dragged back the charred remains of the curtains they found a blackened glass bottle underneath. It appeared from their whispered conversation that someone had stuffed a rag in a bottle of white lightning, lit it, and tossed it through our second-floor window. Only the thick curtains had stopped it from flying into the room and lighting the whole place on fire.

Quite a crowd had formed behind Michael and me, curious as to what had occurred. As soon as the clerk realized this (and the damage such an event might do to the reputation of his hotel) he quickly ushered us to another room at the opposite end of the hall. The porters dutifully followed with our trunks. As we passed the stairs I looked down into the lobby below—and came to an abrupt halt. Standing with his shoulder propped against a marble column near the front doors, fully protected in a circle of sunlight, was Adrien Boucher. He did not look pleased to see us unscathed. Michael tensed when he followed the direction of my gaze, and I firmly squeezed his hand in an effort to keep him from doing anything foolish.

"I should kill that son of a bitch," he swore.

"There's nothing you can do right now," I pointed out. "Don't give him the satisfaction of looking rattled."

Adrien glared at me and then tipped his hat patronizingly in my direction. A moment later a large potted palm fell over, nearly knocking him to the ground. It was a petty bit of magic but in the daylight, in the middle of a crowded hotel, it was the best I could do. I took Michael's arm and propelled him down the hall to our new room, a devious plan forming in my head.

"Put away your temper, darling," I told him. "I've just thought of a way to get rid of Adrien Boucher without anyone having to resort to magic, or vampire powers. It's a little more complicated than just dragging him out and tossing him in the ocean, but it's going to be vastly more entertaining."

"That look on your face makes me nervous," Michael said, grinning. "Whatever your plan is, I like it already."

CHAPTER 20

Devlin had been right when he'd said that guns and gold were the only currency worth carrying in a war. Thanks to General Lawton, the commander of the Confederate forces in Savannah, the next night I strode into Adrien Boucher's plantation house with Michael and ten Confederate soldiers at my back. If I live a thousand years I'll never forget the expression on his face when Boucher came down the stairs and saw me there.

"How did you get into my house?" he demanded. Then he noticed the soldiers and confusion and panic replaced the look of fear his face. "What is the meaning of this?"

"Adrien Boucher," Michael said, stepping forward. "You are hereby served notice that the mortgage on Devil's Island and Kenneway Plantation has been sold to Cin Craven and she is calling in the debt. You can pay it, or you can pack your things and these fine gentlemen will escort you from the island."

"You can't do that!" Boucher railed, as he snatched the deed out of Michael's hand and read it over in astonishment. "You have to give me time to come up with the money!"

I shook my head. "Actually, I don't. And I assume by that statement that you don't have it. Captain Fuller, would you please have two of your men escort Mr. Boucher upstairs and see that he and his family take only their personal belongings from my house?"

The captain was an earnest young gentleman from Savannah and if he thought it was odd that Michael and I had insisted upon doing this at night, he didn't say so. In fact, he seemed to relish the task. I had the distinct feeling that Captain Fuller didn't think much of an able-bodied man like Boucher sitting here safely on his plantation, and not serving his country in uniform. The captain gladly complied with my request and motioned for two of his soldiers to carry out the task. The men had just reached the top of the stairs when Claire came out of one of the bedrooms to see what the commotion was about. Clutched firmly to her bosom was a bronze Grecian urn. Boucher's eyes lit on it as if it were gold.

"She comes with me," he desperately announced. "She's my ward."

Claire drew herself up and glared at him. "I am not. He kidnapped me in London and brought me here against my will."

The men on either side of Boucher narrowed their eyes and took a step closer to him.

"She's addled," Boucher insisted. "She thinks she sees gods and ghosts and the walking dead. She belongs in an asylum, but I just can't bring myself to commit her to such a place. I promised her dear, departed father I would take care of her."

"Oh, balderdash," I spat and turned to Captain Fuller. "He abducted her from her bedroom in the middle of the night and I've come all the way from England, at great personal risk and expense, to retrieve her. She's my cousin."

The captain looked at Claire, who nodded her assent to him, then he looked back at me. Since we'd arrived in Savannah I had been using a bit of glamour to make my naturally blood-red hair a more traditional copper. The family resemblance was well noted by Captain Fuller. He jerked his head toward the soldiers, who man-handled Boucher upstairs to his bedroom to pack his bags. With Boucher out of the way, Claire came rushing down the stairs. I wrapped my arms around her, so glad to finally have what I came for.

"Are you all right?" I asked, anxiously.

"I'm fine," she replied. "He didn't hurt me."

"Why wouldn't you come with me last night?" I demanded. Now that I was satisfied that she was physically uninjured, I wanted to throttle her.

Claire glanced around at the soldiers still lingering in the hall. "I can't tell you now, but when they're gone I'll explain everything. Did you truly buy the whole island?" she asked incredulously.

I shrugged. "I promised your mother I would bring you home. Since you wouldn't cooperate, you left me little choice."

"I'd hoped you would find some way to get us away from him, but I never expected something like that. It must have cost a fortune."

"The money doesn't matter," I replied. "Wait, what do mean *us*? What the devil is going on here?"

Her blue eyes searched my face. "I don't know if you'll believe me," she said, and glanced once more at the soldiers.

Since it was apparent I'd get nothing out of her until we were alone, I ushered her into the parlor. Michael followed us in, closing the doors firmly behind him.

"Claire, I'm a vampire," I reminded her. "Give me some credit for being able to believe things that most people wouldn't, all right?"

She nodded.

"Good," I said. "Now, I want you to tell me exactly what is happening here. What does Boucher want with you?"

"Before I begin," Claire said nervously, "what has my mother already told you?"

I relayed the story that Raina had shared with us, from Claire's disastrous marriage to her abduction.

Claire pursed her lips. "Mother worries more about me than she needs to. After Alastair . . . died . . ." She paused and took a deep breath. "It wasn't that I was damaged, at least not beyond what he did to me physically, and that healed. I was just so *angry* with myself that I had allowed him to do that to me. He wasn't always abusive. In fact, no one could be sweeter than Alastair Gordon when he wanted to be. But it seemed that the longer we were married the less of an effort he made to be kind to me. After his death I spent a lot of time trying to figure out how someone like me—and I do consider myself a very strong-willed woman—could let a man treat her that way and somehow convince herself that it was all right, or that perhaps she deserved it. I'm afraid my family took my mood of quiet reflection for melancholy. I assure you, though, that I am not some wounded baby bird."

"Oh, no," I agreed. "I figured that out last night."

"Well," Claire said, somewhat embarrassed, "there was a good reason for that, which I'll get to in a minute. Mother told you about the young widow who gave me the urn. She didn't just give it to me, she *gave it into my keeping*. She made me responsible for it."

"I still don't understand," Michael said. "Does it truly have that much value?"

Claire shook her head. "It isn't the urn itself, although I daresay that's priceless in its own right. It's what's *inside* the urn that I have to protect."

"And what is that?" I asked.

Claire looked from me to Michael. "This is the part where I'm afraid you'll think I've lost my mind."

I tried to remain calm and simply said, "Why don't you have a little faith in us. What's inside it?"

Claire looked down at the urn, her fingers tightening around it protectively. Then she turned her blue eyes back to us.

"A god of war," she said gravely.

CHAPTER 21

"I'm sorry," I said, very certain I'd misunderstood her meaning. "What?"

"Ares, the Greek god of war," she repeated earnestly.

"She's lost her mind," I mumbled.

"You mean there are human remains in the urn that someone has attributed to the god Ares?" Michael asked.

I nodded to him. That made sense.

"Oh, no," Claire replied sincerely. "I mean the actual god."

Michael and I stared at her for a moment and then I turned to my husband.

"Would you please stay here with her?" I asked.

Then I turned on my heel and exited the parlor, climbing the stairs with a determined stride. When I reached the door to Boucher's room, I didn't even bother to knock.

"Gentlemen," I said to the soldiers, "will you give us a few moments, please?"

The soldiers looked hesitant at first but they must have seen something in my face that made them reluctant to force me to repeat the question.

"We'll be just outside if you need us, ma'am," a private by the name of Riley assured me.

When they'd closed the door I turned on Boucher, who was angrily stuffing clothes into a carpet bag.

"What sort of game are you playing?" I demanded.

"War is not a game, madam," Boucher replied. "I promise you, I am deadly serious."

"You don't actually believe that child is in possession of a war god, do you?"

He looked up, his golden eyes glittering. "I not only believe it. I've seen it."

I shook my head. "Then you're as touched as she is."

Boucher walked around the bed until he was standing mere inches from me. His whole body vibrated with something akin to madness.

"No," he insisted. "You don't understand. I'm the only one who can save our whole way of life. With a god of war on our side, the South cannot help but destroy those damned Yankee aggressors. Once Ares is free, his thirst for blood will know no bounds. We will annihilate the entire Union army."

I shook my head. He honestly and fanatically believed what he was telling me. "Even if what you say is true, you do realize you'd be responsible for the whole-sale slaughter of hundreds of thousands of men?"

He smiled. "Yes, but they'll all be Yankee dead."

"You're mad," I whispered.

"What I am, madam, is destined for greatness . . . and that urn will bring it to me."

"What do you imagine?" I asked. "That you're going to be a war hero, hailed triumphantly in the streets? Statues erected to your name?"

"Something like that," he replied smugly.

"What you're talking about doesn't make you a hero, it makes you a butcher. And I won't allow that to happen."

Boucher reached out and grabbed my upper arms, his fingers digging into my skin and crushing the delicate bronze satin of my gown. Even in his madness, though, he wouldn't look me in the eye.

"This will be mine," he raved, "and mine alone. You will not stop me and neither will your cousin. I'll have that urn or I will burn this plantation down around you all—and once you're dead I'll take it anyway. The choice is yours."

"Yes, you like fire, don't you?" I asked before I pushed him away, my vampire strength sending him flying across the room to land against the wardrobe. He hit it hard enough to break one of the doors in two. Private Riley and his companion heard the crash and came rushing to my rescue.

"Mr. Boucher has had a bit of an accident," I said to

them. Then I turned back to Adrien. "They're more common than you think. Remember that if you ever come after me and mine again."

I sailed down the stairs just as Michael and Claire were coming out of the parlor to see what had happened. With everyone's attention focused on me, we were all startled when the front door clanged open and Mr. McCready rushed in, his ruddy face dripping with perspiration. His gaze traveled quickly over us all until his greedy eyes lit on Claire. Remembering the way he'd dragged Claire into the foyer last night, his covetous eyes roving over her body, my temper flared.

"He goes too," I said firmly to Captain Fuller. "I want him off this island with Boucher tonight."

Mr. McCready's eyes widened. "You can't do that!" he shouted.

"So everyone keeps telling me," I said rather flippantly. "And yet the Merchants and Planters Bank of Savannah and the Confederate Army say differently."

Mr. McCready took a menacing step toward me. Eight Confederate soldiers moved forward but they were no match for the speed of a vampire. Michael was between me and McCready before the man could take another step. Such a move was unwise and drew several surprised looks from the soldiers, but I could hardly fault Michael for trying to protect me.

"The lady has bought this plantation and if she says you go, you go," Michael informed him stiffly. His voice then took on a taunting tone as he said, "But feel free to argue with me about it, if you'd like."

Even though I was standing behind Michael I knew exactly what Mr. McCready was seeing when he looked at him. I couldn't count the number of times I'd seen Michael's face lit up with that arrogant, feral grin. He was confident in his ability to come out the victor in any fight and it either drove a man to back down, or try to prove him wrong. For a moment I thought McCready would be the latter. He did have three times Michael's girth and large, beefy fists that looked as though they'd seen their fair share of brawls. I watched his eyes, though, and I knew the instant he'd made his decision.

"Have it your way," McCready spat. "But I'd like to know how you're gonna to run this plantation without an overseer."

"I'll manage," I assured him with more confidence than I felt, for truthfully I hadn't thought of that until this moment.

"And I suppose it don't bother you none to be throwin' a woman and children out onto the streets in the middle of the night?" McCready asked, gesturing behind him.

A pretty blonde woman, who I assumed to be Mrs. McCready, was standing on the porch just outside the door. In one arm she held a baby with a mass of carrot-colored curls just like his father's. Her other hand was wrapped around the shoulders of a young girl, about eight or nine years old, with long golden braids. I glanced back at Mrs. McCready. For a woman who had just watched her husband being violently threatened by another man, she looked neither frightened nor angry. In point of fact, when she noticed me watching her she quickly wiped a rather pleased expression from her face.

"No," I said. "I would not throw a woman and children out in the middle of the night. You and your family are free to return to your quarters, Mr. McCready. For tonight, anyway."

McCready glanced at Michael triumphantly before he marched out the door, snapping at his wife to follow. The humans undoubtedly missed it, but my vampire hearing picked up his parting shot.

"I hope the slaves rise up and kill you all in your beds," he muttered.

My stomach rolled at the thought and I turned to Michael and Claire.

"I've not only bought a house. I've just bought slaves," I said in horror.

CHAPTER 22

For the next half hour I wandered around the ground
floor of the house, looking into all the rooms and fret-
ting over what I was going to do about the slaves. Claire
had been so afraid that Boucher would try to take her
blasted urn that she had *my* stomach tied in knots. I'd
finally told her to go back upstairs and wait in her room
until he was gone.

"Not as big as it looks from outside, is it?" Michael
asked.

That was true, but it was still a lovely house. Built in
a square with porches and columns on all sides, the interior of both floors had a long hall that ran through the
middle of the house, opening in the front and back with
wide double doors. Off the hall on the ground floor was
a parlor, a library, a dining room, an estate office, and
a servant's bedroom. From the number of doors I'd

counted on the second floor, the house possessed four large bedrooms and one bathroom.

"Where the bloody hell is the kitchen?" I asked Michael.

Before he could answer a prickling sensation raced across my skin. I turned to see Pandora standing in the foyer, watching us. She was dressed as she had been the night before, only tonight her blouse and skirt were black, and the sash and turban were red. Dark magic rolled off her in waves, calling to my own. She smiled as if she sensed it and I had to make more of an effort than I had in a long time to tamp down the darkness that swirled inside me.

"Kitchen's out back in a separate building behind the house," Pandora informed me.

"Whatever for?" I asked.

"You obviously ain't never been in South Georgia in the summertime," she said. "Havin' the kitchen out back keeps the heat out of the house. Also means that if the kitchen catches fire it won't take the whole house with it."

I nodded, looking at Kenneway in an entirely different light. I could see now that the whole house—from the oaks in the yard, to the wide porches, to the central hallways—was designed to maximize the shade, and what breeze there was in the summer, in order to keep the residents cool. It was rather ingenious.

"You keepin' the McCreadys on?" Pandora asked curiously.

"I haven't decided yet, but I'll not be responsible for putting a woman and two small children out without some notice."

Pandora nodded. "Miss Lizzie's a good woman," she said. "Does what she can to make life easier for the slaves. Don't know how she got mixed up with that white trash husband of hers, but she damned sure married beneath herself."

"I take it you don't think much of Mr. McCready?" Michael asked in a tone that made it apparent that he didn't think much of the man either.

Pandora snorted derisively. "Robert McCready ain't much better than an animal."

"If that's the case, then he will be summarily dismissed," I assured her.

Pandora cocked her head to one side. "Why do you care, vampire?" she asked.

"You think that you understand what I am," I replied. "But you don't."

She regarded me with skepticism for a long moment, and then glanced over her shoulder at the sound of a door slamming upstairs and the march of men's boots in the upper hall.

"He'll come back for her, you know," Pandora stated flatly before turning and striding gracefully out the front door.

I moved to stand at the foot of the stairs, watching the soldiers escort Adrien Boucher from his room. He had certainly taken his time collecting his belongings, especially considering he was only carrying two bags. He'd regained his composure, though, and that smooth, arrogant look was once again plastered on his face. He stopped when he reached me.

"This is not over," he promised, and then walked past me with as much dignity as one could have while being evicted.

I didn't like it. He was too calm, too confident. I remembered how Pandora had known we were coming, had known what we were. And her promise that Boucher would be back.

Michael marched past me and stopped Boucher on the porch, clamping one iron fist around the man's arm. Leveling a look on him that I hoped to never see directed at me, he leaned over and whispered, "Don't think I've forgotten that you tried to kill my wife this afternoon. She's inclined to let you walk away, but if I ever see your face again, you'll learn the hard way that I'm not so forgiving."

It suddenly occurred to me that I hadn't seen Boucher's wife earlier tonight and she wasn't with him now. I followed Michael out onto the porch, my gaze roaming over the soldiers standing on the lawn. I wondered if perhaps Mrs. Boucher had left ahead of her husband while Michael and I had been exploring the house, but she wasn't to be seen outside either. I'd just opened my mouth to inquire as to her whereabouts when I caught a brief glimpse of green silk skirts disappearing around the corner of the house. Without a word I followed and when I turned the east corner of the porch, I saw her. A fluffy tabby cat was sitting on the railing and Evangeline Boucher was absently stroking the purring feline as she stared out into the night. I followed her gaze and saw the shadow of a gated cemetery in the distance.

"Mrs. Boucher?" I asked softly.

She was dressed in an off-the-shoulder bottle green silk evening gown and when she turned to look at me I couldn't help but notice that her eyes were the same shade as the dress. Her dark brown hair was parted in the middle and pulled back in artful curls, the style accentuating her heart-shaped face and drawing attention to the exquisite emerald necklace she wore. I could definitely agree with that horrible man in the alley—Adrien Boucher's wife was quite the loveliest woman I'd seen since I stepped off the ship in Savannah.

"What do you intend to do with my plantation?" she asked.

"I don't know," I replied honestly.

She laughed, the sound of it harsh and bitter. "God save me from flighty women who don't know their own minds."

I bristled at that haughty statement. *That odious man certainly hadn't been exaggerating when he'd said she had a tongue like a viper*, I thought.

"Ma'am," I said forcefully, "I'm sorry but I'm going to have to ask you to leave with your husband."

She sauntered forward until she was close enough to look down her nose at me. "Well, I simply can't do that," she replied.

"I realize that it's difficult to leave the home you grew up in, but your husband's treachery has brought you both to this end," I said.

"Oh, honey," she said in a sarcastically sweet tone, "you'll never be able to get rid of me."

"Cin?" Michael called out from behind me.

I turned to see him standing at the corner of the porch, Pandora like a shadow behind him.

"Who are you talking to?" he asked.

I turned back to Evangeline. "Mrs. Boucher obviously doesn't understand what's transpired here tonight and I'm trying, unsuccessfully, to explain the gravity of the situation to her."

"Darling," Michael said worriedly, "there's no one there."

I spun around and looked at him as if he were mad. How could he not see her? He had a vampire's night vision, after all.

"Miss Evangeline's been dead for nearly two years now," Pandora informed me.

Slowly I turned back to Evangeline. She didn't look like a ghost. She looked just as real—and just as solid—as I was.

"She's entirely correct," Evangeline said with a smirk. "And despite the arrogance that apparently runs in your family, I believe I'll enjoy having you and the girl in my house. It's nice to have someone to talk to for a change. As long as you don't run my plantation into the ground with your inexperience, we'll get along fine."

And with that she walked into the house—directly through the parlor wall—and the cat scampered off down the porch. Stunned, I turned back to Michael and Pandora. She was watching me speculatively, as if she was wondering if I had enough magic to see the spirit world. I decided it was best not to let her know how rattled I was by what had just happened.

"Pandora," I said, "I'd like a word with you, if I might."

"Of course, ma'am," she replied respectfully.

"What is your position on this estate?" I asked.

"I'm the housekeeper," she answered. "I got a cabin in the slave village but sometimes I stay in the room at the back of the house, depending on the master's wishes."

I stared into her dark brown eyes, unsure of exactly how to word what I wanted to say. Pandora, though, seemed to understand.

"You're wantin' to know if I'm gonna put some bad juju on you if I'm livin' under your roof," she said.

"No," I said confidently. "I have no fear of that. I know you can feel my magic, Pandora, but you don't have a clue what I'm capable of. You can stay, or you can leave now with Boucher. It makes little difference to me.

If you choose to stay though, I'm warning you now—you do not want to tangle with me."

She met my eyes for a few moments and then she looked down, her decision made.

"Very well," I said. "I'm going to need some paint, black if you have it but any color will do. If you could bring that, then you're free to retire to your cabin for the evening."

"Yes, ma'am," she said.

When she was gone, Michael asked, "Do you trust her?"

"Not a bit," I answered. "In fact, I'm sure I'm going to regret not sending her away with Boucher."

"Then why don't you?"

"Because she has an awful lot of dark magic in her," I replied. "I'd rather have it here, where I can keep an eye on it, than have it jump up and bite us in our proverbial asses when we least expect it."

"Good idea," he agreed as he ushered me through the front door. "Now, would you care to enlighten me as to what all that business on the porch was about?"

"Oh, you're not going to believe this," I said and told him what I'd seen.

"Since when do you see ghosts?" Michael asked incredulously.

"I don't," I replied emphatically as we climbed the stairs to the second floor. "At least I never have before; why should I start now?"

"Maybe it's because of Claire?" he suggested. "After all, her father is a necromancer and you are related to her."

"Which would make sense if she were my ancestor, but she's my descendant," I pointed out. "None of her blood runs in my veins."

I knocked tersely on Claire's door and then walked inside. The room was massive and even the heavy furniture didn't detract from its spaciousness. It was tastefully decorated in blue and white, which nicely complimented the dark wood of the furniture and floors. I found Claire sitting in a window seat, looking as if she'd dressed to match the color scheme in a pale blue gown covered in white lace. She was holding the urn in her lap and staring out at the front lawn, but turned her head sharply when she heard the door open. At first she looked alarmed, though she relaxed when she realized it was only Michael and me.

"Claire, darling," I said gently.

"No," she interrupted. "I'm not crazy. Perhaps I simply didn't explain it as well as I could have. Let me start again from the beginning."

"All right," I said, hoping to hear something this time that made more sense.

"You see these inscriptions here?" she asked, pointing to the urn. "Adrien translated them for me. He's very well educated about Greek and Roman history and mythology. It says here that the god Ares so loved war and bloodshed that during the Trojan War he promised his allegiance to both sides. His meddling and disrespect of human life so angered his sister Athena that she engaged him in battle. Athena, a war goddess herself, gravely wounded Ares and he was forced to flee to Mount Olympus to heal himself. Before long, though, he returned and sided with the Trojans against Athena and the Greeks. Athena was furious at Ares's intervention, which she attributed to nothing more than his love of battle and his will to exact vengeance upon her. She feared his selfishness would prolong the war and cause thousands more lives to be lost, so she went to her brother Hephaestus, the god of metallurgy, and asked him to make something that would trap a god. Now, Hephaestus had no love for Ares, so he created this indestructible urn for Athena. Through trickery she trapped Ares in the urn where he will remain, it says, until he learns to love something more than he loves war, and himself."

"So you and Boucher deciphered that and came to believe that the god of war was trapped in your urn," I said delicately.

"Well, of course not. Don't be silly," Claire replied, and I breathed a sigh of relief. "Adrien, who was in London trying to raise money for the South and convince certain people in the government to side with the secessionists, simply thought the urn would be a lovely gift for President Jefferson Davis. He offered to buy it from me but that poor widow had been so earnest when she'd given it to me that I simply couldn't part with it. She'd said it belonged with me."

"Darling, while this is all fascinating," I said. "I still don't see what it has to do with—"

I paused as a strange, panicked look crossed Claire's face. She jumped up and the urn fell from her lap, landing unharmed on the wood floor.

"Here we go again," said a familiar ghostly voice from across the room.

Claire made a mad dash for her dressing table and proceeded to retch violently into the washbasin. As I held her long hair back away from her face, I glanced over to the big four poster bed and Evangeline, who sat squarely in the middle of it, her skirts billowing up around her as if she were sitting on a green silk cloud.

"Will you get out of here?" I snapped. "This is family business."

"Cin!" Michael exclaimed indignantly.

"Oh, my love, I'm not talking to you," I assured him as I rubbed Claire's back while the spasms continued. "The ghost is back."

"Family business!" Evangeline laughed. "I'll say, honey. She's been doing that nonstop since she got here."

Claire wiped her mouth and sank miserably to the floor. I knelt in front of her while Michael hovered behind me.

"Claire, have you been ill?" I asked, thinking of all

the diseases she could have picked up onboard a ship. "Do you need a doctor?"

"Not now," Evangeline interjected. "But she will in about six months, I'd guess."

Claire glared in the direction of the bed. "Will you shut up?" she snapped.

"What does she mean?" I asked. "Why would we wait six months to . . . oh."

"That son of a bitch!" Michael roared.

Claire winced and looked up at me guiltily.

"There's a boat that belongs to the island moored at the dock," I said to Michael as I stood up. "We can be back in Savannah before dawn. I'll kill that bastard with my bare hands for this."

"Cin, no!" Claire cried. "The baby, it's not Adrien's."

"Oh, I can't wait to hear this," Evangeline said breathlessly as she leaned forward and propped her chin in her hands.

My mind automatically drifted to Robert McCready and I thought I might be sick. Claire struggled to her feet.

"The night after Adrien told me what the markings on the urn meant, I was lying in bed wondering what a war god might look like. On a whim I . . . said something that accidently summoned him. Ares is the father of my baby."

I looked at Michael and he silently met my eyes, both of us obviously thinking the same thing. The girl had been through a traumatic marriage, her husband had been murdered by her mother, and she'd been kidnapped and dragged an ocean away from her home. Clearly the strain of the past two years had been too much for her.

"Adrien was upset that I wouldn't sell him the urn," Claire continued hurriedly. "He came to the house one night when we were supposed to be at a ball. I'd begged off because I wanted to . . . we wanted to . . . well, it had been a long time," she said defiantly. "That's why I was spending so much time in my room. I wasn't brooding. I was with him. Adrien apparently came to steal the urn and saw me summoning Ares. The next night I couldn't get out of going with Mother or she would have become suspicious. When I returned home I found Adrien waiting in my room. He'd tried to call Ares out of the urn and when he couldn't he wanted to know why. I explained to him that only the keeper of the urn could summon him. That's when Adrien drew his pistol and demanded that I relinquish the urn into his keeping. I wouldn't do it. Adrien wants Ares to win this war, and Ares . . . he hasn't seen a field of battle in millennia. I fear what he would do. I'm afraid for him, and for the humans in his path. I told Adrien that if he killed me he'd never get control of the urn. So he took us both, figuring that I would relent eventually. But I wouldn't do it. I won't do it. I haven't even summoned Ares since we left London."

I closed my eyes, trying to keep an open mind while I took in everything she was saying. She seemed so sincere, and who knew better than me that gods really did exist? Could Morrigan have given her control of this deity? I had to admit that however unlikely it was, it was possible.

Michael, however, hadn't thought that far ahead. He took Claire gently by her shoulders and began steering her back to the window seat.

"You've had a rough time of it, lass," he was saying. "Why don't you just sit down and I'll get you a nice dram of whisky?"

"I am not crazy!" she insisted.

"Of course not," he replied.

I know he was only trying to help, but it sounded patronizing, even to my ears. Claire dug in her heels and glared at him.

"Ares, I summon you!" she called out.

A blinding flash of light filled the room and when my eyes adjusted well enough to see again, a man was standing in front of Claire. A very large man wearing bronze armor and looking like he'd just defected from Julius Caesar's army.

"Well, I'll be damned," I muttered.

CHAPTER 23

As it turns out, war gods can be rather hot-tempered. Ares took one look at Claire's flushed and disheveled appearance (which he couldn't have realized was due to the fact that she'd just cast up her supper) and Michael's hands clutching her shoulders and he did not like it one bit. In fact, he drew one massive arm back and knocked Michael clear across the room. By the time Claire and I got our wits together enough to try to stop either of them, Michael had shaken off the blow and drawn his sword.

"Oh, bollocks," I cursed.

Claire and I shouted, threatened, and cajoled but Ares hadn't used the sword strapped to his hip in centuries and Michael's eyes glittered at the opportunity to put his skills to the test with an actual god of war. Neither one of them were going to listen to us, no matter how sensible our pleas might be. Eventually, Claire and I did the only thing we could do—we quickly backed up toward the bed so that we didn't get caught in the fray.

"I told you I wasn't crazy," Claire muttered under her breath.

"Oh, I hope you two stay here forever," Evangeline whispered excitedly. "I've never had so much fun. I can't wait to see what happens next. My goodness, would you look at them!"

I did. It was like watching an angel and a devil do battle. Ares was just as tall as Devlin but not quite as broad. Still, the muscles working in his bare arms were a thing of beauty. His jet-black hair was closely trimmed, as was the Van Dyke beard he wore. His full lips might not have been as attractive on a human, but on a god they were rather sensual.

Michael's dark blond hair, pale skin, and blue eyes contrasted sharply to Ares's dark coloring. He was shorter and, though his body was solidly muscled, it was slender by comparison. Still, my husband's chiseled features, the sharp cheekbones and square jaw clenched in concentration, lent him a chillingly lethal quality the war god didn't possess. For the moment Michael was holding his own and the sight of it made my blood sing.

It wasn't long, however, before it was apparent that the god of war would eventually prevail. Ares got in a lucky stroke that drove Michael down on one knee. The god raised his sword but before he could bring it down across Michael's neck I stepped forward, throwing a ball of magic that hit him squarely in the chest. He staggered back and Michael leaped to his feet just as Ares returned the volley, sending what looked like a streak of blue lightning in my direction. I ducked and it hit the wall behind my head, scorching a large black mark across the white paint.

"Ares!" Claire shouted and he snapped his head around in her direction. "Do not throw a god-bolt at my cousin! And while you're at it, quit trying to kill her husband. He was only comforting me, nothing more."

Ares turned curious eyes to me and rubbed his armor-plated chest. "What manner of god are you?" he asked.

I shook my head. "I'm not a god. I'm a witch . . . and a vampire."

"Vampire . . ." he mused. "Ah yes, one of Morrigan's creatures."

I nodded.

He glanced over at Michael. "This explains why you fight so well," he said before turning his attention back to Claire. "They do not harm you, *filati*?"

"No," she said smiling. "They do not harm me. They're family."

Ares stepped forward to go to her but stopped short when Claire held her hand up.

"Oh, God," she said miserably and rushed back to the washbasin.

"Not again," Evangeline groaned as she moved off the bed. "If all the fun is over, I have better things to do."

With that she walked through the bedroom wall and disappeared. Ares's eyes widened in surprise.

"What place is this?" he asked. "And why is Claire ill?"

Holding Claire's hair back with one hand, I looked pointedly over my shoulder at Michael.

"She's not ill," Michael informed him. "She's pregnant. With your child."

"My child?" Ares whispered in disbelief. "I'm to be a father?"

Before I knew it the two men were laughing, hugging, and slapping each other on the back as if they'd both managed to accomplish something no other man in the history of the world had ever done. I dipped a cloth in the pitcher of water and pressed it to the back of Claire's neck.

"Could you two find somewhere else to do that before I turn you both into weasels?" I snapped.

When Claire had recovered enough to wash her face and rinse her mouth out, Ares came striding up behind her, grinning like an idiot, and swept her into his arms.

"Oof," she muttered. "Breast plate."

He glanced down and the armor disappeared. I arched a brow at the incredibly lovely expanse of muscled chest it revealed. Ares spun her around (which I wasn't sure was wise) and she laughed and smiled up at him. Then his lips came down to claim hers in a kiss that made me blush.

"I believe our work here is done," Michael said as he ushered me quickly from the room. "For tonight, anyway."

When he closed the door behind us, I turned to him and wrapped my arms around his waist.

"I don't know about you," I said, laying my head on his chest, "but I'm exhausted. Even my brain hurts."

He laughed. "I will say this—life with you is never boring."

Unfortunately, he was right.

CHAPTER 24

As tired as I was, I couldn't sleep. Pandora had been gracious enough to find us some white paint and, as much as I hated to do it, Michael and I had painted over the glass on the three large windows and the double doors that led to the porch off the master bedroom. We'd gotten it finished just before dawn and, with the room now vampire-friendly, had fallen gratefully into bed. Michael was asleep in minutes but my mind was whirling with the events of the past few weeks and I couldn't shut them out.

Claire was obviously unharmed, though I didn't know how I was going to explain her current condition to her mother. That, however, was not what I was worried about. We still had at least a week, possibly two depending upon how long Devlin and Justine stayed in Jamaica, until we could leave. That was a lot of time for Boucher to make his move. I could boot him off the island, I could even post a guard at the dock, but he'd lived here for a long time and if there was another way to get onto this island he would know it. I had taken everything from him and I didn't for a moment believe that he would let that go without seeking some sort of vengeance. I didn't worry about a face-to-face confrontation. It was what damage he could do, especially in the daylight hours, before we knew he was here, that concerned me.

And, as if that weren't enough, I now owned slaves. Not for long, certainly, but I had to deal with that issue as well. Of course I would free them, but I had no idea what that entailed. I was relatively certain that the law required a bit more than me just waving my hands and saying "you're free." Perhaps Mr. McCready would know how one went about emancipating one's slaves. And once the slaves were gone, who would work the plantation's fields? It would be difficult to hire the labor needed to accomplish such a task with most of the able-bodied men away fighting the war. Perhaps I should simply close up the whole plantation and sell it after the war was over.

These thoughts and the various scenarios that followed them floated through my head for hours. I tossed and turned and glared at my husband, wondering how he could sleep so soundly with everything that was going on. Around noon I finally fell into a fitful slumber . . . which lasted for exactly two hours, until I woke with the nagging feeling that someone was watching me. I cracked one eye open.

"Why are you here?" I asked Evangeline, who was standing beside the bed, staring down at me with something that resembled contempt on her face.

"Because when I refused to tell Adrien where my father had buried the last of his gold, he pushed me down the stairs and I broke my neck," she replied.

"I'm sorry," I said sincerely. "But what I actually meant was, why are you *here*?"

"Cin?" Michael asked groggily.

"Go back to sleep, darling. It's only Evangeline," I told him.

He groaned and rolled over.

"What you should be asking is why are Pandora and Ulysses still here," Evangeline said as she floated a few feet away and perched on top of one of our trunks, which the soldiers had been gracious enough to carry upstairs for us last night.

"Who is Ulysses? And why shouldn't they be here?" I asked.

"Ulysses is Pandora's husband and they don't belong to Kenneway. They came here from New Orleans with Adrien. They're his slaves. He should have taken them with him, yet he didn't. She's dangerous, that one, and entirely loyal to Adrien. You should put her on the boat to Savannah immediately."

I opened my eyes and stared up at her. "I don't understand you people. How can someone be loyal to a man who claims to own her?"

"Because she's not only his slave," Evangeline informed me. "She's his daughter."

That got my attention. I sat up quickly, pulling the sheet up around my body. "Well," I said, "that puts a bit of a different light on it. Are you sure?"

"Quite sure," she said bitterly. "I'd always had my suspicions about those two, but a familial relationship was not what I thought Adrien had with her. I learned the truth, more than I wanted to know, one night after Adrien came back from England with the girl. He and Pandora were arguing, so I decided to eavesdrop. Adrien wanted Pandora to give Claire some sort of potion that would make her compliant, but Pandora refused. She said it might kill Claire and that she wouldn't be party to murdering an innocent white girl. Adrien was furious and told Pandora that if the north was successful in the war, our whole way of life was doomed."

"What did she say to that?" I asked. I couldn't imagine a slave being too upset about that prospect.

"Pandora said, 'It ain't your way of life though, is it? You ain't a planter and you never was. You stole this life with all those pretty lies you told to Miss Evangeline. And she believed it all, thinkin' you came from some big River Road plantation. She never would've looked twice at you if she'd known you weren't nothing but a poor cracker with a handful of slaves you couldn't afford to feed.' And then he hit her and told her that if she wasn't his daughter he'd beat her bloody for speaking to him that way." Evangeline laughed bitterly. "What a fool I was to believe his lies, when he was nothing more than a simple schoolmaster's son who'd won a small farm and a few of slaves in a river-boat card game in his youth."

I rested my chin on my knees, thinking. I felt sorry for Evangeline, but my mind was eased somewhat about Pandora. I didn't trust her for a moment, but at least I didn't believe she would poison Claire's breakfast.

"So, do you agree with me about getting rid of her?" Evangeline asked impatiently.

"Not quite," I replied. "My friend Devlin often says that you should keep your friends close, but your enemies closer. If Adrien is planning something, Pandora will know about it. And you, Miss Evangeline, are the perfect spy."

She smiled at me. "I am, aren't I?"

I nodded. "Keep an eye on her. If you see or hear anything suspicious, let me know immediately."

"I can't promise anything," Evangeline warned me. "Pandora practices the voodoo and she seems to be able to feel it when I'm around. But I'll do whatever I can to see that Adrien gets what he deserves. It was bad enough that he murdered me, but to have lived all these years with a man who was nothing more than a lie . . . it's more than a woman should have to bear."

"He'll get what he has coming to him," I said. "I'm willing to let him walk away, but I know he won't be wise enough to do so."

Evangeline nodded. "I'm glad you came here. Perhaps now I'll finally have my vengeance," she said. "And speaking of vengeance . . . what the devil have you done to my windows?"

I spent the next twenty minutes explaining to a ghost what a vampire was.

CHAPTER 25

Near dusk Michael woke me with a whispered question. "Are we alone?"

I cracked one eye open and glanced around the empty room. "Yes," I replied. "Blessedly alone."

He gathered me in his arms and rolled onto his back, pulling me on top of him.

"And what would you like to do this evening, my beautiful wife?" he murmured as his fingers trailed lightly back and forth across the bare skin of my back.

It was quite apparent what my amorous husband had in mind. Smiling wickedly, I slid slowly down the length of him, trailing kisses along the muscled ridges of his chest as I went.

"Well," I said, as I worked my way down his stomach, "I should check on Claire and see how she's faring this morning."

I swirled my tongue around the indentation of his belly button and then moved lower.

"And then we must decide what to do with Mr. McCready," I added, passing my lips lightly down his rock-hard shaft, my hot breath making him quiver beneath me. "But what I *really* want to do is . . ."

"Yes?" he whispered raggedly.

I ran my tongue up the length of him and then swiftly sat up and pasted a thoughtful expression on my face.

"Take a walk down to inspect the slave village," I said lightly and bounded off the bed.

I made it halfway across the room before a feral growl erupted from the general direction of the mahogany four-poster. With a giggle I sprinted for my clothes, which I'd left draped across a chair next to the wardrobe. I'd almost made it when Michael slammed into me, his momentum carrying us both forward so that I had to put my hands up to brace against the impact. He grasped my wrists and spun me around, pinning me to the wall.

"Tease," he scolded.

I smiled. "You know you love it."

"I'll show you what I love more," he replied.

Grasping my hips, he lifted me. I wrapped my legs around his waist as he drove into me, insistent and unyielding. A shudder of pure pleasure ripped through my body and I dug my fingernails into the corded muscles of his neck.

"On second thought," I said, gasping for air, "this is a *much* better idea."

CHAPTER 26

It was early evening when Michael and I came downstairs to find Claire sitting by herself in the dining room, eating supper.

"Good evening, Claire," I said. "That's a lovely gown."

Even though our coloring was similar, that particular shade of mauve would have looked virulent on me. On Claire it looked stunning.

"Why, thank you, Cin," she replied cheerfully. "But I can't take credit for it. Adrien didn't allow me to pack any of my belongings, so it's a blessing that Evangeline and I are nearly the same size." She looked down at the dress and adjusted the bodice a bit. "If I hadn't lost so much weight, it would fit perfectly."

"This is her second helping," Evangeline announced as she drifted into the room through the wall. "I don't know why she bothers when it's all going to come back up anyway."

"Because I'm starving," Claire said. "And for someone who didn't have anyone to talk to before I arrived, you'd think you'd be a little more pleasant."

"Evangeline," I murmured to Michael, since he was obviously confused by the one side of the conversation he could hear.

"Claire?" Michael asked. "You didn't, ah, inherit any of your father's abilities, did you?"

Claire smiled at him over her teacup. "Do you mean can I control the undead? No, I can't, but I have always been able to see ghosts."

"That must have been disconcerting as a child," I said.

"Not really. Mostly they're just lonely spirits who can't, or won't," she said with a meaningful glance toward Evangeline, "move on to where they're supposed to be. I always enjoyed talking to them, though I'm afraid the villagers thought I was a little daft."

Poor Claire, I thought. It often amazed me that anyone born into my family had a shred of sanity left by the time they reached adulthood.

"Do you think Pandora has any more of this wonderful blackberry jam?" Claire asked, changing the subject. "I can't get enough of these biscuits. I could eat them all day."

I looked at the heaping plate in front of her and shook my head. I remembered that when I'd first seen her I'd been worried because she was so thin. I'd thought perhaps Boucher wasn't feeding her properly. Now it was obvious that she was eating like a horse, she just couldn't keep anything down.

"Is it normal to be that sick?" I asked.

Evangeline and Claire both shrugged so I turned to Michael.

"Well, how would I know?" he said.

Pandora came into the dining room carrying a bowl of fresh strawberries and another pot of jam. "First strawberries of the season," she announced.

"Ask her," Evangeline said. "Pandora attends all the births on the island. If anyone would know, it would be her."

"Pandora, how long can Claire expect the baby to make her so ill?" I asked.

She didn't seem surprised that I would ask her such a thing. "Well, now, that depends," she replied. "Most times it only lasts a few months. There's some women don't never get sick, and then you gots women like Miss Lizzie who threw up for nine months straight with both her young'uns."

I looked sharply at Claire, whose eyes had grown round with horror.

"I am not going to be like this for another six months," she said emphatically.

Pandora laughed. "Well now, Miss Claire, you ain't the one who decides that."

Before any of us could comment on that horrendous

possibility, a door in the rear of the house slammed and the sound of running feet drew our attention. Michael and I rose quickly from our chairs as the dining room door burst open and the little McCready girl came sliding to a halt in front of Pandora.

"Pandora," she said breathlessly. "Mama said she saw you picking strawberries this afternoon!"

Michael and I looked at each other and sat back down, relieved. Pandora reached out and tweaked one of the girl's long golden braids.

"Miss Ginny, where are your manners?" she scolded. "How many times I have to tell you not to run in the house?"

"I'm sorry, Pandora," Ginny said. Then she peeked around Pandora's skirts at us. "I'm sorry for running in the house," she said earnestly.

I nodded at her. "That's quite all right, Ginny."

The girl smiled and then beamed up at Pandora. "Can I have some strawberries now?"

Pandora grasped Ginny's hands and turned them over. "Not with those hands you won't. Where you been playin', child? With the pigs? How you ever gonna find a husband if you can't keep the dirt out from under your nails?"

Ginny snatched her hands back and placed them firmly on her hips. "I'm never gettin' married, Pandora. You know that."

I chuckled sadly at her vehement protest. If I'd had

a father like hers, I rather thought I'd be sour on marriage too.

"Well, you might be changin' your mind about that
one day," Pandora insisted. "In the meantime, why don't
you run on out to the kitchen and wash up, and then
maybe I'll get you some strawberries."

Ginny whooped in a very unladylike manner and
dashed from the house. Pandora shook her head and
followed the girl out. I watched Pandora go, thinking
what a paradox she was. She seemed to genuinely care
for Lizzie and her daughter; she even seemed to like
Claire. But there was a cloud of dark magic around her
that made me very nervous, especially since I didn't
know whether or not she might use that magic to help
Adrien Boucher. I found myself wanting to like her,
and yet at the same time I fully expected her to do something awful. I popped one of the strawberries into my
mouth and chewed thoughtfully.

Claire laughed. "I hope I have a little girl just like
Ginny."

"Speaking of children, where might the father of
yours be?" Michael asked.

Claire frowned down at her jam-covered biscuit.
"Ares had to go back," she said sadly. "I can summon
him, but I can't control how long he gets to stay. Sometimes it's only an hour, sometimes it's a whole night.
You never can tell."

"Can't you just call him back out again?" I asked.

"It only works once a day," she replied. "Twenty-four hours from the time he goes back into the urn I can try again."

"Do you love him?" Evangeline asked.

"Yes," Claire said softly. "With all my heart."

"Oh, Lord help you, girl," the ghost muttered before she got up and disappeared again.

I tended to agree with her. I couldn't imagine how such a relationship was ever going to work. Then again, I'd fallen in love with a vampire, so who was I to judge?

CHAPTER 27

It was a lovely night. The spring air was cool and perfumed with the scents of honeysuckle, pine, and jasmine. As I stepped off the back porch, I heard a loud thump and curse from inside the house and laughed softly to myself. Claire had coerced Michael into bringing down several more trunks full of Evangeline's dresses from the attic. My poor husband always did have a hard time saying no to a Macgregor woman. He would catch up with me as soon as he could, but for the moment I was enjoying the relative quiet of a solitary stroll.

I walked around the detached kitchen, following a stone path that led to a stand of trees behind the house. Ginny's tinkling laughter spilled from the open windows of the kitchen and I smiled as I passed. From inside I could hear Lizzie McCready's soft southern drawl as she explained the intricacies of canning preserves to her daughter. I continued along the stone path, through the trees, and out into a meadow bisected by a wide dirt road. Assuming that somewhere in the darkness ahead this road would meet up with the main road that ran from the docks to the house and would continue on to the slave village, I turned and followed it.

After several yards I was surprised to come upon a lovely white cottage with a beautiful garden planted out front. A young slave girl of about twelve or thirteen sat in a rocking chair on the front porch, holding a baby that I recognized as Robert and Lizzie McCready's youngest child. The girl eyed me cautiously. Perhaps it was because I was a stranger, or perhaps it was the fact that I was wearing boots and breeches that unnerved her. She herself was wearing a pretty beige dress printed with blue flowers.

"Good evening," I called to her with a smile. "That's a lovely dress."

She flushed and glanced down, a shy smile on her face. And then both of us nearly jumped out of our skin when the front door slammed open and Robert McCready strode out onto the porch. He was wearing work boots and beige pants held up over his portly belly by suspenders. The white cotton shirt under them was stained with sweat. I eyed the pistol holstered at his waist and wondered why he would feel the need to wear such a thing in his own home.

"Cassandra," McCready said in his big booming voice. "Why don't you take the baby inside?"

He laid his hand lightly on her shoulder as he said this and I did not like the way she flinched from his touch, or the fear that was suddenly quite obvious in her eyes. Cassandra clutched the baby to her chest and scurried past him into the house. I stood at the base of the steps and looked up at Robert McCready, not liking him any better tonight than I had last night.

"Mrs. Craven," he said, raking one hand through his halo of carrot-colored curls. "I think perhaps we got off on the wrong foot, you and me."

"Perhaps we did, Mr. McCready," I conceded. "But I think not. If you'll come up to the house after supper tomorrow night, we can discuss the future of your employment on this plantation."

Which is going to be very limited, I thought as I turned and walked away.

I could feel two sets of eyes on me as I continued down the road. One was Robert McCready's and the other belonged to a slave boy, perhaps a few years older than Cassandra, who was hiding in the trees near the cottage. I had no idea what he was doing there but, since I wasn't willing to call McCready's attention to him in order to find out, I passed him by without acknowledging his presence.

When I reached the end of the meadow the road continued on for another hundred yards or so through the woods, spilling out into a large clearing ahead. About halfway there I felt a small prickling of dark magic move within me and I glanced to the left. The trees had been cut back here, for what reason I couldn't guess. There was something supernatural at work out there, though. While my curiosity was piqued, my good sense got the better of me this time. Pandora, and perhaps this very island, made my dark magic hard enough to control. I did not need to go searching for further ways to tempt it.

The road eventually emptied into a long, narrow meadow. Two rows of cabins stretched down its length, lining the drive. The slave village was quiet and dark tonight; the only sign of life was a wizened old woman who sat on the front porch of one of the cabins. She glanced quickly over her shoulder toward the edge of the field behind her cabin. I followed her gaze and found myself drawn to another path leading into the woods, this one not made of stone or packed earth but carved into the forest by the treading of many feet.

I was perhaps twenty yards in when I first heard the beating of the drums. They called to me with almost as much strength as Raina's summoning spell, drawing me deeper into the woods. I could see a clearing up ahead, a large bonfire burning in the center of it. When I stepped from the trees my eyes widened at the sight in front of me.

The drums were beating and it appeared as though most of the village was dancing around the great fire. In various stages of undress, they twirled and gyrated in wild abandon, singing and calling out to the heavens as they moved. I walked forward, enthralled by the sight, and something deep inside me stirred to life with the rhythm of the drums. The dark magic that I'd always felt from Pandora was here—almost a living, breathing thing in the meadow.

A large man was the first to notice my presence. He caught Pandora against his chest as she danced past him and pointed in my direction. I'd never seen her like this. The omnipresent turban was gone and her hair hung loose down her back. She looked like some sort of pagan goddess, her body glistening with sweat. Pandora and I stared at each other across the clearing, then she picked up her blouse from the grass where she'd discarded it, pulling it on as she walked toward me. Every instinct I possessed screamed for her not to come any closer, but I couldn't seem to bring myself to move. With each passing moment the darkness inside me built, looking for a way out. It suddenly occurred to me that I was hungry. *It* was hungry, and I wasn't strong enough to hold it back. The rhythm of the drums picked up and I watched the dancers, lost in the ecstasy of their movements. All those bodies, filled with blood. Not in some far-off city, but right here a few feet away.

And then Pandora was in front of me, her dark eyes filled with an understanding she couldn't possibly have. I looked at the smooth skin, the veins pulsing just below the surface. But Pandora was filled with black magic. I couldn't take her blood. Drinking from a dark mage was what had gotten me in this trouble to begin with.

"I can't be here," I said breathlessly and with every ounce of strength I had left, I turned and fled.

"Miz Craven!" Pandora called after me and I could hear her running to catch up with me.

Please don't. I said to myself over and over. *Please don't follow me.*

I skidded to a halt when I reached the slave village. Through the pounding in my head I could hear a pounding of a different sort—footsteps running on the packed earth of the road. For a moment I thought that Michael had somehow sensed my distress and come for me, but the sound wasn't heavy enough for a grown man. Moments later the boy I'd seen hiding outside the McCreadys' cottage burst into the clearing. Pandora came up beside me, grabbing the boy's shoulders as he skidded breathlessly to a stop in front of us.

"What is it, Hector?" she asked urgently.

"My sister . . ." the boy gasped. "Mr. McCready . . . you said to tell you if . . ."

Pandora spat a particularly violent curse and took off running in the direction of the overseer's cottage. I stood there staring at the boy, his hands on his knees as he tried to catch his breath. In mythology, Hector's sister was Cassandra. I thought of the way Robert McCready's eyes had roamed over Claire's body the first night I'd met him, the way Cassandra had flinched at his touch tonight.

"Oh, bloody hell," I cursed, and took off after Pandora.

CHAPTER 28

It didn't take me long to overtake her. My vampire speed was no match for a human and I arrived at the cottage in a fraction of the time it would take Pandora to get there. I stopped and listened, not wanting to frighten the entire household just in case the boy had been mistaken. At the sound of a muffled cry from inside the house I gained the porch in one leap and kicked in the front door. Unfortunately for Robert McCready, I now owned Kenneway Plantation and every building on it. It meant that I could enter his house without an invitation, and enter it I did.

McCready jumped up from his crouched position over the sofa. In one glance I took in Cassandra's tear-stained face and her pretty flowered dress, which was now torn at the shoulder. The girl jerked the hem of her dress down and scooted backward until she was wedged against the arm of the sofa, as far away from us as she could get. Her large, dark eyes darted from McCready to me and back again. Robert McCready held his hands up in front of him, his ruddy face flushed with exertion or embarrassment, I wasn't certain which.

"This ain't what it looks like," he said.

With a growl of outrage I sprang forward and grabbed the front of his shirt, throwing him bodily through the front door. He flew through the air, landing on his back in the front yard. I turned to Cassandra.

"Did he hurt you?" I asked, barely able to contain my anger long enough to not frighten her further.

She shook her head. "No, miss," she replied softly. "Not this time."

Not this time. By the gods, she was only a child and a slave girl completely under his power, as well. In that moment whatever control I had over my temper and my black magic snapped. I felt the darkness rise up inside me, turning my brown eyes to black with its power. I stalked to the edge of the porch and looked down at Mr. McCready as he picked himself up off the ground.

"You bitch!" he spat. "What I do in my own house ain't none of your damned business!"

"What you do with my people is entirely my business, Mr. McCready," I replied coldly.

I'm not sure what he saw in my eyes, but whatever it was it made him reach for the pistol at his hip. I smiled and sprang from the porch. The darkness inside me swirled jubilantly at the sound of his screams. It fed on blood and death, growing stronger as I tapped the vein in McCready's neck and his hot blood spilled into my mouth. I could have killed him with black magic alone. For a moment I let the darkness travel across my skin. It would be so easy to simply hold him down and allow the magic to suck the life from him, leaving nothing more behind than bone and ashes. But tonight the darkness wanted blood and just this once I wasn't adverse to playing with my food. Several times I let him up, let him fight me as well as he was able. I never even felt any blows he managed to land.

From all directions around me I began to hear voices and somewhere deep inside I realized that a situation which should have been over quickly and quietly was beginning to draw a crowd.

"She's gonna kill him."

"Don't reckon that'd be a bad thing, do you?"

"Should we try to stop her?"

"How you think we gonna do that?"

Dark hands reached for me but my magic pushed them back, scattering bodies in several directions. The sheer force of it made me pause and I glanced up from Robert McCready's struggling body. I saw Pandora standing on the porch, watching me with speculative interest. Cassandra stood wide-eyed next to her, her ripped dress hanging drunkenly off one shoulder. I saw Lizzie rushing up the steps, herding Ginny into the safety of the house. The guilt I felt at mauling that child's father right in front of her pushed the darkness down, giving me a brief moment of sanity. And in that moment Michael hit me like a locomotive. We tumbled backward and the feel of his body against mine quelled the darkness inside me like water being thrown on a fire.

"Jesus Christ, Cin," he yelled. "You could have killed him. What were you thinking?"

I pushed him off of me. "He was molesting a child, Michael. I didn't think. I just . . . I lost control and I couldn't have stopped it even if I'd wanted to."

The anger that radiated from my husband shifted its focus from me to McCready. We both stood and I grasped Michael's wrist, afraid he might be tempted to finish what I'd started.

"Spawn of Satan!" McCready said raggedly as he struggled to his feet, one hand pressed to the wound on his neck.

I hadn't been gentle. Instead of two puncture marks, it looks as though a rabid dog had gnawed on his flesh. Breathing harshly, he pulled his hand away and looked at the blood. Then he looked back up at me with indignant fury in his eyes. With shaking hands he jerked the pistol from the holster at his hip. Someone screamed as Michael instinctively placed his body in front of mine.

"I'll send you back to hell, where you belong!" McCready shouted and raised the gun.

I flinched as a loud report filed the meadow. A look of shocked crossed Robert McCready's face before he pitched forward and fell dead at our feet. We all stared in disbelief at Lizzie McCready, who stood on the front porch of her cottage, a Henry rifle pressed to her shoulder. For a few quiet moments she looked dispassionately down at the body of her husband. Then without a word she numbly turned, took Cassandra by the hand, and led her back into the house, closing the door behind them.

CHAPTER 29

Michael and I stood silently with half a dozen slaves, unsure of how to proceed.

"They ain't gonna bring the law down on Miss Lizzie, are they?" Hector asked, glancing nervously back at the cottage.

Michael looked down at the boy. "No," he said firmly. "I'll take his body out to sea and get rid of it."

"Why can't we just bury him here?" I asked, not liking the idea of Michael out in open waters where he could be spotted by Union patrols, especially with a murder victim in his boat.

"Because," Michael said, "eventually someone will wonder what became of him. It's best if his body is not found on this island with a gunshot wound in his chest. This way he just disappears and, should anyone ask, we can truthfully say we don't know where he is."

"All right," I agreed. "Do you want me to go with you?"

"No," he replied. "You go back to the house and stay with Claire. I'll handle it."

He effortlessly slung McCready's body over his shoulder and headed off toward the dock. With the excitement over, the slaves began to disperse, melting quietly into the shadows. I stood, watching Michael's retreating figure until I could no longer see him. *I'll handle it*, he'd said. Only it had sounded more like *I'll clean up your mess*. A frisson of dread went through me at the conversation that I knew was coming when he returned. Wearily, I sat down on the steps of Lizzie's porch. Looking down at my blood-stained shirt, I grimly wondered what my face must look like. Pandora moved silently from the shadows of the porch to come and stand in front of me.

"How long you been pretendin' that black magic ain't inside you?" she asked.

I opened my eyes and looked up at her. "Since 1818," I replied honestly, too tired to argue that it was none of her business.

She whistled and shook her head. "You must be one strong woman to deny half of who you are for that long."

"The dark magic is nothing more than an infection," I said. "It is not who I am."

"'Course it is," she insisted. "You're a powerful

bokor. You serve the loa with both hands." She reached down and grasped my wrists, turning my hands over in hers, palms up, to illustrate her point. "One is for the darkness and one is for the light. Together you find balance and harmony. Take one away, and you tip the scales."

I pulled my hands from hers. "There is nothing harmonious about what's inside me."

She laughed. "You're some arrogant vampire, you know that? You think you're the only one in the world got demons? Unless you're God Almighty, we all got some darkness inside us, Miss Cin. You can't walk through this world without it. Now, you got two choices: you can get you a big ol' shovel and bury it deep . . . but it's gonna rot inside you and taint everything you touch. Or you can accept what you are, put it on like a coat, and wear it proudly."

I looked up at her dubiously. "You don't understand what the magic can do when I lose control of it."

"Oh, I understand the black magic a whole lot better than you do right now," she said. "It ain't nothin' to be scared of. Let me explain it a different way. That darkness is like a hungry, stray dog. You get scared of it and you kick it away, well, it's likely to bite you. But you bring it inside and feed it, make a friend of it, and it'll be yours forever." Pandora looked down at me and shook her head sadly. "You got to feed that black dog, Miss Cin, before it turns nasty and bites you."

She turned and strode off toward the village and I sat there for a long time, wondering if she was right.

CHAPTER 30

I was sitting in the middle of the four-poster bed in the master suite when Michael finally returned near dawn. Wordlessly, he stripped off his clothes, sodden with blood and sea spray, and tossed them into a pile on the floor. Gloriously naked, he walked across the room and looked down at me, running one hand through his dark blond hair. It was a gesture of frustration he'd picked up from Devlin over the years and any hope I'd had that I might be able to seduce him into waiting until tomorrow to talk about this went right out the window. Instead, I scooted over and pulled back the covers.

"I haven't seen you lose control of it for a long time," Michael said carefully. "You could have killed him, you know."

"But I didn't," I said, more harshly than I'd intended.

"Only because I was there to stop you, Cin. What if I'd been too late?"

"Then I'd say he deserved it."

Michael took my chin in his hand and turned my face to his. "That isn't your call to make," he said softly. "We execute vampires who kill humans, Cin."

"I know well what we do, Michael. I've been covered in the blood and death of it for nearly half a century." I shook my head. "Yes, I lost control of the darkness. I don't know why. Perhaps it has to do with the black magic that seems to permeate this island. But what do you want me to say, Michael? I'm sorry I wasn't stronger. I'm sorry that others witnessed it. I'm sorry if that makes what we're trying to do here harder. But if you expect me to say that had I killed him I'd be crying in my whisky right now, you're going to be disappointed."

"I'm not disappointed in you, Cin. I'm scared for you."

I took a deep breath and laid back against the pillows. "I know," I said wearily. "I didn't mean to snap at you. It's just that I'm so tired of having to be *in control* all the time. It's . . . it's bloody exhausting, Michael."

I told him about my conversation with Pandora and what she'd said about the black magic. The minute I saw the expression on his face I wished I'd held my tongue.

"You aren't actually considering this, are you?" he asked in astonishment. "You aren't seriously telling me you're thinking of taking the advice of a woman steeped in black magic, who may or may not be in league with the man who kidnapped your cousin and tried to burn a hotel down around us?"

"I know what she is, Michael, but you can't deny that it makes some sense."

"Sure," he said incredulously, "and I would tell you to give it a whirl if your magic made butterflies out of bees or turned water into whisky. But it is deadly, Cin. I've seen you in the throes of it. You don't know what you're doing and you could hurt a lot of people in the process. Remember the conversation we had at Ravenworth, and a thousand times before, about Gage and Edinburgh?"

I narrowed my eyes at the way he said *a thousand times before*. "I'm sorry I'm such a trial to you."

"Don't you ever think that," he said hotly. "It's just that I know you and I know the guilt you carry, despite your brave words about Robert McCready just now. You've killed humans, Cin, evil humans, and their deaths still weigh on you. Think about how you would feel if you hurt any of the innocent people on this island. If you try this and things go badly, how are you going to stop it before it harms, or even kills, someone you care about?"

I wanted to be angry with him for not having faith in me, but I couldn't. He was right.

"I don't know," I replied honestly. "I'm just so tired, Michael. I'm tired of fighting a war against myself."

He gathered me in his arms and kissed my neck.

"I know," he said softly. "I love you, Cin, and if I could take that burden from you, I would."

It was meant to be comforting, I knew that, but his words only made me feel worse—like I had some sort of disease he wished he could cure. I closed my eyes and we lay there in silence, listening to the birds chirping as dawn broke across the island.

CHAPTER 31

Supper the following evening was a quiet affair. Michael sat silently at my side. He'd been following me around like a disapproving shadow all evening, as though he were waiting for me to snap and start massacring people. It was already getting tedious and I had at least another week and a half such nonsense to look forward to until Devlin and Justine returned. I wasn't certain if Claire sensed the tension between us or if spreading blackberry jam on her biscuits truly required that much concentration, but finally she broke the silence.

"What are you going to do with the plantation, Cin?" she asked.

"I have some thoughts on the matter," I said eagerly, "but I don't know the law here well enough to know how, or even if, such things can be accomplished."

"We were going to ask Mr. McCready's advice on the subject," my darling husband felt the need to add.

"Well, good riddance to bad rubbish, I say," Claire declared. "Just out of curiosity, what are you going to tell Lizzie about—"

Claire bared her teeth and held her hands up, curling her fingers in a claw-like gesture that I assumed was meant to look like a vampire. I rolled my eyes and pressed my palms to my forehead.

"I have no idea," I said.

As if summoned by my thoughts, Pandora entered the dining room to announce that Lizzie McCready wished an audience.

"I suppose we might as well get this over with," I muttered. "Pandora, please make Mrs. McCready comfortable in the parlor and tell her I'll be there shortly." Michael and I rose, and I looked across the table at Claire. "When you're finished, you're welcome to join us if you'd like."

She nodded eagerly and proceeded to spread blackberry jam across another biscuit.

CHAPTER 32

When we entered the parlor Lizzie McCready was standing next to the fireplace looking nervous and uncomfortable. Belatedly I realized that my appearance tonight probably did nothing to put her at ease. Since the debacle of the previous evening, I'd given up any pretense of being human. I'd dropped the glamour I'd been using to keep my hair copper-red, returning it to my natural scarlet. And had I known Lizzie was coming tonight I would have dressed more appropriately in one of my lovely evening gowns instead of my breeches and boots, but there was no help for it now.

"Mrs. McCready," I said, "I'm glad you came. Please, sit down."

"Mrs. Craven, I am eternally grateful to you for saving Cassandra last night. But I have two questions that I'll be needing answers to," Lizzie blurted out, as if she'd practiced her speech and now wanted to get it over with as quickly as possible. "First, I need to know, for my childrens' sake, what you intend to do about . . . what happened last night."

"I don't believe there's anything *to* do about it, do you, Michael?" I asked, knowing that she was wondering if we were going to turn her over to the authorities in Savannah for murder.

Michael sat down, lounging negligently against one arm of the sofa. "No," he agreed. "I don't believe there's anything to be done about a man who would run off in the middle of the night and abandon his wife and children."

Lizzie stared at us for a long moment as understanding dawned on her. Then she let out a shaking breath and some of the color returned to her cheeks.

"And your other question?" Michael asked.

She swallowed hard and shifted her gaze from him to me. "I know what sort of a monster my husband was," she said.

I nodded. "And now you'd like to know what sort of a monster I am."

Lizzie sank down on the wing chair across from me. "I suppose so," she said, "though I would have never put it so indelicately."

It took quite a bit longer to explain to Lizzie what we were than it had to Evangeline. Mostly because, after what she'd seen last night, it was difficult to convince her that we were neither evil, nor were we going to harm her or her children. It helped that halfway through the conversation Claire joined us, sitting on the sofa between Michael and me without a care in the world. Lizzie had come to know Claire in the weeks she had been here and Claire's trust in us helped to ease Lizzie's fears.

That is, until Claire felt compelled to announce, "And as long as we're confessing our sins, I'm pregnant and Ares, the Greek god of war, is the father of my child."

Lizzie's eyes widened and she looked at the lot of us as if we were all deranged.

I patted Claire's hand. "Perhaps we should move the topic of conversation on to something a little less supernatural. Mrs. McCready—"

"Please," she interrupted, "call me Lizzie. I think we know enough of each other's secrets at this point to dispense with formality."

"Lizzie, I have to decide rather quickly what I'm going to do with this plantation," I said. "I'm hoping that you can give me some guidance."

Lizzie looked startled, but pleased. "I'd be honored to offer whatever advice I can," she said.

"The very first thing I want to do is free the slaves," I announced.

Lizzie shook her head. "You abolitionists are all alike. You have high ideals but none of you understand the reality of what you're doing."

I raised my eyebrows.

"Perhaps you could enlighten us, then?" Michael suggested.

"All right," she said. "First of all, even if you wanted to, you can't do it. It's illegal to free a slave in the state of Georgia. You can make a black person a nominal slave, which basically means they are allowed to live and work as a freedman under your guardianship. There are many of them in Savannah. But there are bonds and monthly taxes that must be paid for this and the cost of doing such a thing for every slave on this island would be prohibitive."

"How prohibitive?" I asked.

She gave me a figure that, even with my financial resources, I was disheartened to hear. "Well," I said, "is it illegal for me to take my slaves to a free state and emancipate them?"

"No," she conceded, "but say you do take them up north and free them, what are they supposed to do then?"

"Whatever they want to do, I suppose," I replied.

"See, this is what I'm talking about," Lizzie said. "Just on this plantation alone, that would mean taking nearly a hundred colored folks who have little education and no marketable skills except as farm laborers and dropping them in the middle of some strange Yankee state. Where are they supposed to live? What are they supposed to do for work? How are they going to feed their families? Most of these slaves have never been off this island." She shook her head. "Life might eventually be better for them in a few generations but right now, for these people, to set them free means unimaginable hardship and possible starvation."

"Not to mention you're going to bankrupt my plantation!" Evangeline hissed in my ear, making me jump.

"Don't you have someplace else to be?" I whispered fiercely.

"Pandora's in the kitchen with Ginny," the ghost said. "What's happening in here is a whole lot more interesting."

Michael glanced sharply at me and, figuring out what was going on, drew Lizzie's attention away from me and continued the conversation.

"While it would be possible to pay the fees and taxes to make them nominal slaves," Michael said. "I dislike the idea of giving that substantial an amount of money to a state that perpetuates slavery. I have every faith that by the time this war is over Mr. Lincoln will free them all anyway. I think we simply need to figure out how to proceed between now and then."

"I honestly do appreciate the sentiment behind what you're trying to do," Lizzie said. "I just don't want to see them worse off than they are now. These are good people. I care about what happens to them. As you're well aware, Robert was not always . . . the kind of overseer he should have been. These men and women are hard workers and their labor feeds and clothes us all, black and white alike."

"And you want to throw them out into the street," Evangeline complained as she flopped down in the chair next to me. "Where, if they're lucky, they might be able to scratch out a living as subsistence farmers. And this house is going to fall down around our ears because there's no income to support it."

"I'm not throwing anyone out into the street," I said under my breath. "Now, would you be quiet and let me think?"

"Good luck with that," Claire mumbled.

"Well, I don't know," Evangeline responded sarcastically. "If I do, are you going to come up with something better than this abolitionist tripe?"

"Are you all right, ma'am?" Lizzie asked.

"I'm fine," I assured her. "Just talking to myself. It helps me think."

Lizzie didn't look like she believed a word of that, but she was polite enough to not say so.

"How much do you know about what your husband did on this plantation?" I asked her, an idea taking form in my head.

"What do you mean?" she asked suspiciously.

"I don't mean any of his more nefarious activities," I assured her. "I mean what his duties were, how many acres are under cultivation, what should be planted and when. That sort of thing."

"My father was the overseer on one of the largest plantations in South Carolina," Lizzie said proudly.

"I daresay I know more about how one should be run than Robert did."

"Excellent," I said. "How would you like his job?"

Four pairs of eyes looked at me in astonishment.

"Cin, are you sure you've thought this through?" Michael asked.

Evangeline laughed heartily. "Yes, I can see Lizzie McCready now, out tromping through the fields in her hoops, directing the slaves!"

At that I turned to Evangeline and said out loud, "Would you give me credit for having some common sense and hear me out?"

Lizzie shifted uncomfortably in her chair. "Perhaps I should come back later after the two of you have had a chance to talk this over," she suggested.

I shook my head. "No, that wasn't directed at Michael. I was . . ." I sighed, and couldn't think of a single reason that, after everything else we'd confessed, I shouldn't tell her about Evangeline too. "Lizzie, what would you say if I told you that at this very moment the ghost of Evangeline Boucher is sitting next to me, harping in my ear that I'm running her plantation into the ground?"

Lizzie blinked at me and then burst into laughter. "I'd say that sounds exactly like what Miss Evangeline would be saying right now."

CHAPTER 33

It took at least an hour to come to an agreement about the future of Kenneway Plantation that would satisfy all of us. It turned out that I owned over sixteen hundred acres, nearly half of which was under cultivation, mostly in Sea Island cotton. While that was a good cash crop, it wouldn't feed hungry mouths if the war and the economy went badly. Lizzie eagerly offered her suggestions on how many acres we should devote to food crops and which ones to plant. She then launched into a dissertation on the benefits of crop rotation, which bored me silly but did reassure me that I'd chosen that right person for the job. Even Claire had a few good ideas, when she wasn't out leaning over the porch railing, vomiting on the azaleas. Evangeline wasn't thrilled but at least what I offered was better than she had expected of me.

It was after nine o'clock by the time we'd put together

a workable plan. Nevertheless, I called for Pandora and asked her to have someone hook up a wagon and drive us all to the slave village. The boy Hector took the reins and Michael boosted Claire up so that she could sit comfortably next to him. The rest of us—me, Michael, Pandora, and Lizzie—perched in the back. As we rolled past Lizzie's cottage I noticed the lamps were well lit, Cassandra waiting with the children for Lizzie's return. When the wagon reached the little clearing in the woods I felt my skin tingle as it had last night. I shivered and Michael put one arm around me reassuringly. For the first time tonight I was glad of his overprotectiveness, and I leaned into him. He always seemed to be able to pull me back from the darkness.

"What is that?" I asked, nodding toward the clearing.

"The slave cemetery," Lizzie answered.

My magic had never stirred in proximity to a cemetery before. Perhaps it had something to do with my new ability to see ghosts. *Or perhaps it isn't me the dead are responding to*, I thought, with a glance at Pandora.

When we reached the village, Hector pulled all the way down the road, stopping in front of the last set of cabins. People spilled out of their houses, filling the lane in front of me. Somehow I had expected to find only young people, strong enough to work in the fields, but here were whole families—old men and women, their children, and grandchildren. I was suddenly struck with the enormity of the responsibility I now held to see that I did right by them. One man in particular caught my eye, standing at the back of the crowd. I had seen him at the bonfire last night with Pandora. He stood head and shoulders above the rest of the group, his bare ebony arms the size of tree trunks crossed over his barrel chest. There was a look of suspicion and distrust on his face that I sincerely hoped to alleviate.

I stood up in the back of the wagon and Lizzie came to stand at my right side. Michael moved up behind me and laid one had gently on my shoulder. Motioning to Pandora, I called her to stand at my left. She was the housekeeper up at the plantation house, the midwife for the village, and, I was certain, the one people went to for their medicines and charms. She had influence here and I wanted her by my side while I said what I'd come to say.

"My name is Cin Craven," I announced loudly. "My husband Michael and I have bought this plantation. As I'm sure you know by now, Mr. Boucher and Mr. McCready are no longer in residence on this island."

I watched the large man as I said this and saw a smile of satisfaction twitch at the corners of his mouth.

"My husband and I will be returning to England soon, but before we go there are some changes I want to implement on this plantation. Hard times are coming and I want this island to be able to support itself when that happens. I have faith that plantations such as this one, run by slave labor, will soon be a thing of the past. What I want to build here is a model for the future. It was my intention to give each of you your freedom, but I'm told that it's not as simple as that. For those of you who wish to travel to a free state and gain your freedom that way, I will help you do so, both logistically and financially. For those of you who wish to stay here, I will make you this promise: when the Union wins this war, or the laws change and I can legally grant you your freedom, I will do so immediately. At that time, if you wish, you can leave this island and I will settle a sum of money on you to help you start a new life. It won't be easy. A war is raging in your country. Right now it's far away, but soon it will be on your doorstep. When it's over, this country will no longer be the same and I fear life in it will be very hard for some time. You can take the money and make your way in the new world that's opening up out there, or you can stay on Devil's Island. If you decide to stay, here is what I'm offering:

"From this day forward you'll see fair pay for a day's work. You'll also share in the profits from the crops that are raised here. A new village will be built with finer cabins for you all. And there will be a school-house where your children can receive an education," I added, coming up with that last idea on the spur of the moment.

"Educating them is also illegal," Lizzie whispered.

"Oh, honestly, who's going to tell on me?" I whispered back. Aloud, I continued, "Mrs. McCready will move into the big house and she will take on the job of overseer of this plantation."

There was a murmur through the crowd and the big man in the back spoke up. "With all due respect, ma'am, you expect Miss Lizzie to be out in the fields in the sweltering heat, supervisin' the field hands?"

"No, I don't," I said. "Mister—?"

The crowd parted and the big man strode to the front, stopping directly before the wagon.

"Name's Ulysses," he replied, crossing his arms over his chest again.

Of course it is, I thought. "Mr. McCready's former job will now be handled by two people, working together as partners," I explained. "Mrs. McCready will handle the bookkeeping, the payroll, the plans for the crops, and the sale of the harvest. Basically, she'll be responsible for everything Mr. Boucher and Mr. McCready did except for the direct supervision of the workers. For that job we've chosen a man I think you'll all approve of."

"And who might that be?" Ulysses asked, looking unimpressed.

I smiled down at him. "Well, that would be you, sir. Mrs. McCready assures me that I could find no better man to do the job. When she moves into the big house, you and Pandora may have her cottage as part of the compensation for your new position."

A hushed silence fell over the crowd. Even Pandora was staring at me as if I wasn't speaking English.

"War is an ugly thing," I said, filling the silence. "It often brings disease, starvation, and poverty. This island is so beautiful and I don't want that ugliness to touch it. You have the resources available, both from the land and the sea, to feed yourselves well and still make a profit. Perhaps this plantation will never again see the grandeur that it once did but, by making Devil's Island as self-contained and self-sufficient as possible, you can survive this war and the hard years that will follow much better than most of the country will."

The silent crowd looked at Ulysses, and Ulysses looked at his wife. I turned to Pandora, confused. I had expected a better reaction than this but she was staring at me as if I'd suddenly grown a second head.

"Ma'am," she said slowly, "Did you just promise us our freedom, land, and wages, and give my husband a white man's job?"

"That about sums it up," I said. "So, what do you think?"

She shook her head, bemused, then a big smile crept over her face. She grasped my hand and the moment she touched me I could feel her magic call to mine. The darkness stirred like a nest of snakes in my belly. I quickly pulled my hand away, but Pandora didn't seem to notice.

"I think we're gonna show those white folks that we can make this the best damned plantation in the south!" she shouted.

A cheer went up through the crowd and Ulysses reached up and plucked his wife down from the wagon, twirling her around while she laughed. People gathered around Lizzie asking questions, which she readily answered. It was clear that she cared for them and they held a great amount of respect and affection for her. I turned in Michael's arms and smiled up at him.

"You did a good thing here, lass," he said.

I leaned up and kissed him. "*We* did a good thing," I said. "I'm almost glad that getting Claire back didn't go as smoothly as we'd planned." I gazed out over the village, imagining what it would look like in a year, or ten. "We fight evil, which is a great and noble calling, but it's nice for once to do something that has more than a theoretical impact on the future. I want to build something here and I want to come back over the years and watch it grow and change. I want to do for this island what my ancestors did for Glen Gregor."

"A safe haven in a time of war," Michael said. "Well, if that's what you want, *mo chridhe*, then that's what you shall have."

CHAPTER 34

It was very late when Hector finally returned Michael, Claire, and me to the house. I sailed happily into the parlor and began looking for a decanter, intent on toasting to the success of our plans.

"Oh, for the love of Danu," I muttered as I opened a rococo cabinet to find nothing in it but a tea service. "Why is there no liquor in this house?"

"There is somewhere," Claire said. "I've seen Adrien drink it. But on the last Sunday of every month Reverend Simmons comes out to the island to preach and he always stays for supper." Claire wrinkled her nose. "That was the only meal I've had on this island that I didn't enjoy. Adrien hides the liquor when the reverend comes, but I don't know where."

I rolled my eyes and shouted to the ceiling, "Evangeline, come down here please!"

"I will not be summoned like some lackey," the ghost hissed as she popped into her favorite chair.

As if she somehow knew where her mistress would be, the tabby cat dashed into the room and hopped up on the arm of the chair. Absently, I reached down to pet her.

"*Don't!*" Claire and Evangeline shouted simultaneously, but it was too late.

The cat spit at me and raked its claws across my hand, leaving four deep furrows in my skin. I jerked my hand away and the cat's back hunched up, her long hair standing on end as she growled and spat a final warning. Before I even thought about what I was doing, my canines lengthened and I hissed back at her, showing her that I had much larger teeth than she did. The tabby turned tail and flew out of the room as if the very hounds of hell were chasing her.

"That was rude," Evangeline said.

"She started it," I protested.

Claire laughed. "For future reference, never attempt to touch Vendetta."

I looked at Evangeline. "You named your cat Vendetta?" I asked incredulously.

The ghost smiled wickedly. "Originally she had another name but as a kitten she took a prompt and particular dislike to my husband. He couldn't leave any article of clothing lying around or she'd pee on it. I have no doubt that she would have followed me to an early grave except for the fact that no one but me can lay a hand on her."

I narrowed my eyes at the ghost. "Keep your cat off my clothes."

"Of course," she said, a little too sweetly.

"While I'm sure the conversation is fascinating," Michael interrupted, holding up an empty glass, "could we return to the topic of Reverend Simmons and the liquor?"

"That fat, judgmental bastard," Evangeline spat. "Oh, it's behind the books on the third shelf, dear. Yes, you should hear the way the reverend goes on about *the evils of lust and demon liquor*, and how we have to *eradicate sin from our lives*."

She said this in what I assumed to be an exaggerated impression of the reverend and I chuckled as I reached behind the books.

"I mean, really," Evangeline went on, "does he honestly expect that all his fire and brimstone speeches are gonna do a lick of good? Sin is fun. If it wasn't, no one would do it and he'd be out of a job!"

I retrieved a bottle filled with clear liquid from the back of the bookshelf. I certainly hoped it was vodka and not gin. Pulling the cork out, I took a whiff.

"Oh dear Goddess!" I exclaimed. "What is this stuff?"

"White lightning," Evangeline replied. "You'd think I would have realized from his taste in liquor that Adrien wasn't anything but white trash, now wouldn't you?"

Gingerly, I took a sip and indeed it burned like lightning all the way down. I exhaled, feeling as though my mouth were on fire.

"That might actually be strong enough to get a vampire drunk!" I said and passed the glass to Michael.

As I poured another glass for myself, I caught Claire glancing at the clock on the mantle. I knew she was counting the minutes until she could summon Ares from the urn. I handed her a glass of water and raised my own.

"To the new Kenneway Plantation, may it thrive and prosper," I toasted.

"We still have a great deal to accomplish in very little time," Michael said, "but I think we made an excellent start tonight."

"Speaking of time," Claire said. "When will your friends' ship return for us?"

I looked questioningly at Michael.

"I don't think we can expect them back in less than a fortnight," he replied. "If they can't make it before the full moon, we may have a longer wait than that."

"Would that be such a bad thing?" Claire asked, speaking more to herself than to us. Then she glanced again at the clock.

"No," Michael said. "But I'm sure you're eager to get home and see your family."

"Yes," Claire said, swirling her water around in her glass. "I would love to see my family again."

Michael didn't seem to notice it, but I did. Claire said

she was eager to see her family, but not that she was eager to return home. I wondered why.

"I believe I'll retire for the evening," she announced.

"Good night, dear," Michael said and kissed her on the cheek.

"Yes, good night," I replied thoughtfully.

I looked at Evangeline, who had been unusually quiet. She was watching Claire's retreating figure with the same worried expression I was.

CHAPTER 35

Near dawn I took a glass of my beloved whisky and opened the porch doors of the master suite, intent on taking a quick stroll before bed. I stopped before I'd even taken a step outside and turned to Michael.

"You're stalking me," I said accusingly.

"No, I'm not," he replied, looking a bit embarrassed.

"Yes, you are. I haven't had a moment to myself in the last twenty-four hours. I feel fine, Michael. Pandora is in the village and there's nothing out there on the porch that's going to set me off. If, as we've always assumed, the black magic reacts to my temper," I said, poking one finger into his chest, "you're pushing it."

He rocked back on his heels and looked at me incredulously. "You wouldn't hurt me."

"Well, no, I wouldn't," I agreed, somewhat deflated. Then I narrowed my eyes at him. "But if you ever want to see me naked again you need to back off and give me some room to breathe."

"Fine, but if you eat someone, don't blame me," he said wryly.

"I won't," I snapped and firmly shut the door in his face.

I stifled a giggle and shook my head. *By the gods, what a mess,* I thought.

Tomorrow night Michael and I would have to take the boat into Savannah. He hadn't fed since we left the city. It wasn't necessary to drink every night but it wasn't a wise idea to go too long without blood either, especially around humans you don't wish to drink from. A hungry vampire cannot be trusted, Devlin always said. Apparently right now I couldn't be trusted either and, rightly or wrongly, that fact galled me.

Perhaps things would be better if I were away from the island and its dark influences. Michael and I would go back to Savannah, spend a night or two, and drink our fill. Hopefully Devlin and Justine would be back from Jamaica before we needed to feed again. We would, of course, have to take Claire with us, one of us staying with her at all times to guarantee her safety.

I took a sip of whisky and tried to push everything out of my mind. Instead, I watched the breeze play through the branches of the oaks. The Spanish moss swayed gently in the trees, the crickets chirped in the garden, the frogs in the salt marshes called to each other . . . and in that brief moment I had the overwhelming feeling that all was right with the world. Or perhaps it was just a feeling that it would all work out well in the end. It simply felt good to stand here on the porch of a house that I owned and feel as though I once again had some roots.

I knew that what I did as a member of The Righteous was worthwhile. I helped to make the world a safer place, for vampires and humans alike. Still, the constant traveling and unending violence that was my life sometimes took its toll. I'd occasionally wondered, lately, what it would be like to give all that up for someplace like this. When you live forever, though, you need something more than peace and quiet to occupy your time. If I didn't have to get Claire home to her worried family, I would have enjoyed staying here for a while. But I knew that eventually this would not be enough, for me or for Michael.

I took a large sip of whisky and began to wander, trailing my fingers across the porch rail as I went. The porches encircled the whole house and I walked along, enjoying the view from different angles—the oak-lined drive in the front, the little cemetery on the east side of the property, the kitchen and gardens at the rear of the house. I turned the last corner to find Ares standing on the porch, his arms braced against the railing, looking out on the northern horizon.

He closed his eyes and inhaled deeply. "There is war to the north."

It made me slightly uncomfortable the way he said *war* in the same tone I might say *whisky* or *chocolate*.

"Yes, there is." I looked off into the distance, following his gaze. "Are you going to go?"

He shook his head. "I cannot. The urn, my prison, is here and that is where I must remain. I've lost the power to shift through space and time."

"Do you *want* to go?" I inquired, which was probably the more pertinent question.

"I am a god of war," he replied simply.

"That isn't what I asked."

He turned and looked behind us, through the open porch doors to Claire's bedroom. She was asleep, her copper curls spread across the crisp white sheets. Even in slumber she looked content, happy.

"I think . . . I think I would rather stay here, with her."

I cocked my head to one side. Claire was a pretty girl, but I'd thought that perhaps his interest in her was no more than that of a man who had been without the company of a woman for a very, very long time. Now I wasn't so sure.

"She is . . . complicated," he said, "and more damaged than she seems. Even so, she doesn't hold back her heart. She gives it away with both hands. I've never known anyone like her. She is . . . the light to my darkness. Can you understand that?"

I nodded. "More than you know."

"Before she learned how to free me, I would sit in my prison and sometimes I would hear her crying at night. She doesn't cry anymore and that . . . pleases me."

I started to say that it pleased me as well, but there was a sudden flash of light and he was gone. I blinked.

Well, I thought, *Claire did say that they had no control over when the urn reclaims him.*

I walked into Claire's room and picked up the urn from the nightstand. Quietly, I laid it on the bed next to her and pulled the covers up around her.

"You should leave her here," Evangeline said softly from behind me.

I turned to see the ghost lounging against the porch door, looking in at Claire.

"You're just saying that because when we leave you won't have anyone who can see you or hear you anymore," I told her.

Evangeline shrugged. "I'll freely admit to being selfish enough to want her to stay for just that reason, but I was actually thinking of what was best for her. What's she to say when she comes home with no father for her baby? At least, not one that she can publicly claim."

"We'll think of a plausible story," I assured her, though I didn't know what that might be.

"Another dead husband? Or maybe some louse who married her and then ran out on her? Those are pretty much your only options. If she's lucky they'll pity her into an early grave. Most likely no one will believe a word of it and they'll tear her to pieces."

"The people of Glen Gregor are not like that. Her mother would not allow such behavior."

"All people are like that," Evangeline said bitterly. "If they don't do it to her face, they'll do it behind her back. She'd be better off here, where no one will look down on her or the child."

I turned back to Claire. She'd been through so much in her young life already. I knew deep down that Evangeline was right and it tore at my sense of honor. I'd made a promise to Raina to bring Claire home safely, but what if home wasn't the safest place for Claire?

CHAPTER 36

I was blissfully asleep—basking in a lovely dream involving me, Michael, and a pot of melted chocolate—when Evangeline's screeching woke me.

"He's here!" she was shouting in my ear. "Adrien is in Claire's room and Pandora's screaming that he's killed her! Hurry!"

I jumped out of bed and grabbed my dressing gown, throwing it over my naked body as I shouted for Michael and ran out the door. As I rushed down the hall I could clearly hear Pandora and I cursed myself for sleeping so soundly for the first time in weeks.

"You couldn't get it from me so you bought it off some no-good bokor in Savannah, is that it?" she was yelling. "How much did you give her? How much?"

Unmindful of the sunlight that splashed across the wood floors only a few feet from me, I grasped the knob of Claire's bedroom door. It was locked but the bolt was not strong enough to keep out an angry vampire.

"She's with child and you've probably just murdered them both!" Pandora shrieked as I burst into the room.

Claire was lying on the bed, her eyes open. I ran to her, grateful to see the rise and fall of her chest.

"Claire!" I pleaded, "Can you hear me?"

Boucher grabbed Pandora by the wrist and dragged her toward the balcony door.

I turned my head to them. "Let her go or I'll kill you where you stand," I said.

"She's mine and she comes with me," Adrien sneered.

Pandora turned defiantly to him. "I'm yours no longer, *master*. And you'll burn in God's own fire for what you've done to that poor girl."

Michael ran into the room, wearing nothing more than a pair of breeches that weren't entirely buttoned and clutching one of my knives in his fist. He took one look at Adrien and rushed forward. Adrien shoved Pandora toward him and dashed out onto the balcony. Michael drew up short, stepping back from the pool of sunlight with a menacing growl.

Adrien smiled and he seemed to possess more teeth than a man ought to. It only added to the oily quality he had about him.

"I told you this was not over," he said triumphantly.

Just as Michael drew back his arm back, Claire started moaning and thrashing about. It was enough to throw his aim off a few inches. The blade sank into Boucher's shoulder instead of his heart. He staggered backward, looking down at the knife in shock. It was one of my favorites and I was thankful when he pulled it free and dropped it to the floor. I would have been more thankful if he'd fallen with it. Instead, he crawled awkwardly over the porch railing, dropping down into the azaleas below with a prolific amount of cursing.

Too late I saw the satchel he had slung over one shoulder. I looked at the empty spot on Claire's nightstand.

"Oh, for the love of Danu! He's got the urn!" I cried. "We have to stop him."

Michael turned and motioned toward the sunlight. "How do you propose we do that?"

I growled in frustration. "There has to be someone here who can shoot that blighter!"

"The men are all in the fields," Pandora said. "We're the only ones near the house and I don't know how to shoot no gun."

"It's too late anyway," Michael said, looking out the window. "We'll have to go after him tonight and hope he hasn't gotten far."

I should have done something, I thought angrily. Perhaps if Michael hadn't had me so tied up in knots about my magic, I would have reacted as I should have. At the time, however, my first concern had been for Claire. I looked down at the girl lying helpless in my arms.

"Pandora, what did he do to her?" I asked.

She walked to the bed and picked up an empty vial lying on the floor. "Jimson weed," she said. "And I don't know how much."

"What does it do?"

Pandora shook her head and rushed to the get the washbasin. "Depends on how much he managed to force her to swallow," she replied as we rolled Claire over and made her throw up into the basin. "And how much we can get outta her before it's too late. Most likely, she's in for a bad few days, but she'll be fine . . . if it don't kill her."

"That's not encouraging," I snapped, wondering how much of the poison was even now rushing through Claire's blood.

"It ain't meant to be," Pandora said. "Jimson weed is bad stuff. When Miss Claire first came here the master wanted me to give it to her. It'll make a person mindless, see? Compliant. He said it would save the time of tryin' to wear her down. I wouldn't give him any, though. You never know how someone's gonna take to it and I wasn't gonna be responsible for killin' no white woman."

"Make her compliant," I murmured. "So that she would give him possession of the urn."

"Someone under the spell of jimson weed would give away possession of their own soul, if it was asked of 'em," Pandora said ominously.

"What do we do?" I asked.

Pandora shook her head. "Make her comfortable and keep her from hurtin' herself. Only thing you can do. She's probably gonna lose that baby, though."

"Oh, God," Michael groaned.

I looked down at Claire, who was still muttering incoherently. *How much bad luck can one person have?* I wondered miserably.

I turned to Pandora. "Have someone go to the dock. I sent Hector out there to keep watch. Either Adrien didn't come ashore there, or . . ."

Pandora's eyes widened. "I'll see it done, ma'am."

Michael came to stand next to me. "What would you like me to do?"

"There's not much either of us can do until dark, other than get dressed and wait," I replied. "Michael, do you think this is why Morrigan sent us here? To prevent a god from affecting the outcome of the war?"

"I honestly don't have a clue," he replied.

I sighed and stroked Claire's hair. "I just don't understand Morrigan's motives. She gives this thing of power to my cousin . . . for what purpose? Even if she knew what would happen, I can't believe she has a care one way or the other about who wins this war. What did she hope to gain by such an act?"

Michael shook his head. "Who can understand what the gods know, what they see? You'll drive yourself mad trying to figure it out. Here's what I do know: the High King's laws forbid us from meddling in the affairs of humans, particularly in human wars. Whatever the outcome of this one is destined to be, I think it should be won or lost by the humans, not by Ares or Morrigan."

"You don't think a war god has a place on the field of battle?"

"Before I met Morrigan I never believed in more than one god. There was God, and that was it. Perhaps she and the others are His intermediaries. Perhaps they're simply extremely powerful beings who have no connection to the divine at all. I don't know. But I have seen war and it's horrific enough without some minor deity using it as a playground."

I nodded, completely agreeing with him. "So we'll stop Boucher and get the urn back because that's what we all believe is the right thing to do. And if that wasn't Morrigan's intention, then she bloody well should have been more specific."

CHAPTER 37

The hours until sunset were agonizing. We moved Claire into the master suite, where Michael and I would be safe from the sun's deadly rays as we watched over her. She quickly slipped into delirium, not knowing any of us, but speaking to her mother and Ares as if they were sitting at her bedside, carrying on a conversation with her. She was flushed and feverish but, as Pandora had promised, entirely compliant when I asked her to sit up and drink some water for me. Once she thought Alastair was with her and she screamed and thrashed about until I was forced to hold her down so that she wouldn't harm herself.

Often she wanted to get out of bed and take a walk. A couple of times I allowed it, helping her up since she could barely stand by herself. Throwing her arm over my shoulder, I held her so that she wouldn't fall. Like two drunks we staggered around the bedroom. She seemed to think that she was walking in the gardens at Glen Gregor with her mother.

"I do miss you, Mama," she said to me, her speech slurred. "But I'm happy at Kenneway. I wish I could stay forever. No one there looks at me like I'm odd." She laughed. "They're all much stranger than I am."

My heart broke for her. She seemed so lost, like she didn't have a place in the world, and I had begun to feel a motherly urge to protect her. I slid her back into bed and pulled the covers up over her as she continued her one-sided conversation. Soon, though, she was speaking nothing but incomprehensible gibberish. I was pacing the room when Pandora knocked softly and entered.

"Ulysses and the men are nearly finished with the boat," she announced.

Adrien had tried to buy himself a head start by putting a hole in the plantation's only boat. Thankfully, it was still tied to the dock and Ulysses and some of the field hands were able to pull it ashore and mend it.

I watched as Pandora lifted Claire's head and slipped a small cloth bag tied with a string around her neck.

"What is that?" I asked.

"It's *gris-gris*," Pandora replied. "Good magic. It will help her get better."

"Feeling guilty, are you?" I asked.

Pandora stilled.

"I know you came from New Orleans with Boucher. You should have gone with him when he left, but you didn't. You stayed here to help him. You knew when he was coming back, and what he intended to do."

She turned to me, looking both guilty and defiant. "I knew he wanted the urn."

"Do you have any idea what that thing is?" I asked.

"I know its powerful magic and he wants it. And you're right; I did do whatever the master asked of me. But that was . . . before. Miss Cin, you was vampires and he was . . ."

"Your father," I stated.

She looked surprised for a moment, then nodded. "What would you have done?"

I really couldn't argue with that. I probably would have done the same.

"I knew he was comin' today," she admitted. "I was afraid if I told you, you'd kill him. Whatever he is, he's still my daddy. So I came up to Miss Claire's room this morning, intendin' to be here when he came. I was gonna stop him, tell him to go on and leave us all in peace. But he was already here. He came earlier than he was supposed to—probably because he knew I'd never let him give her that jimson. I promise, Miss Cin, if I'd known what he meant to do to her . . ."

"All right," I interrupted, feeling that she was genuinely sorry for what she'd done. After all, had it not been partially my fault? I had expected something like this and I should have been more vigilant. "But, Pandora," I said, "you need to make a choice here and now where your loyalty lies. I'll set you free and send you wherever you want to go, but if you stay on this island—"

"I swear by the sword of Ogoun I will never fail you again," she vowed.

I had no idea who Ogoun was, but I understood her meaning and that was good enough for me. Shortly after Pandora left, Michael came to say goodbye. We both looked down at Claire. She'd been resting peacefully for a while but now she was stirring again, tossing her head and mumbling.

"The baby?" Michael asked.

"She hasn't lost it yet," I replied.

I wondered, briefly, if that was necessarily a good thing. She would be returning to Glen Gregor soon, with a baby in her belly and no husband on her arm. It would not be easy for her, or the child. Still, I had seen how happy she was and I knew it would kill her to lose this baby. Therefore, I prayed for its safety as hard as I prayed for her life.

Michael crossed the room and I watched him strap his claymore to his hip with grim determination.

"That doesn't look like the older, wiser Michael," I said, trying for some levity though I was actually terribly worried.

Michael tucked a pistol into the waistband of his pants. "No, we're doing it the old-fashioned way this time," he said as he pulled on his coat.

"How far can he have gotten in an afternoon?" I asked.

"Darling, the railroad runs out of Savannah. He could be anywhere by now. Ulysses is going to take us into Savannah in the boat. Are you ready?"

I shook my head. "Michael, I can't go with you. How can you ask me to leave Claire when she's in this condition?"

"How can you expect me to do anything else?" he countered.

"Michael, I know you don't think I can control the black magic, but I can. What happened with McCready . . . well, I wasn't prepared for how strong it would hit me, but I am now. It's rather like walking around with a loaded gun. I didn't think that I needed the safety on, but now I know that I do. It won't be an issue again."

"The magic isn't the only thing that concerns me, Cin. It could take days, or even weeks, to track down Boucher and you need to feed. I know your tender heart and I know you won't drink from Lizzie or one of the slaves. You'll sit here by Claire's bedside day and night until you're half mad with hunger. And then what do you think will happen?"

Well, it was apparent that Michael thought I would go mad and smite the entire island with black magic.

"I promise to have Ulysses take me into Savannah tomorrow night," I vowed.

Michael crossed his arms over his chest and raised one eyebrow. I scowled and glanced at Claire, mumbling

listlessly in her delirium. I was a horrible liar. No
matter how good my intentions were, Michael was
right. I would take care of Claire before I would take
care of myself and we both knew it.

"Let me put it to you this way," he informed me. "I
won't leave here without you. If you're concerned about
Pandora, I'll ask Lizzie to move into the house and care
for Claire until we return. Now, do you want the urn
back or not?"

I looked down at Claire. Could I truly justify her life
being more important than the thousands that Ares
might take at Boucher's command? She herself would
tell me to go, if she were able.

Michael reached out and touched my hair. "I also
think it would do you good to get off this island for
a while," he said softly.

My temper flared at that. I knew he meant well but it
seemed that every time I turned around recently he was
treating me like I was defective, dangerous, or deranged.
I longed for him to look at me again and see only his
wife, not a deadly weapon.

"Fine," I agreed and pushed past him. I reached the
wardrobe and opened the doors, numbly pulling out
practical clothing for such an endeavor. "But you realize that if she dies alone, I'll never forgive you," I said
softly.

"I'd rather bear that burden," he replied, "than have

you have to live with the guilt if things go wrong and
no one is here who can stop you."

Frustrated, I brushed a tear from the corner of my
eye. Truly, sometimes I did not deserve him.

CHAPTER 38

I was angry. I was angry at Boucher for what he'd done to Claire, angry at myself for not stopping him when I'd had the chance, and angry at Michael for not trusting me enough to leave me alone on the island. It was not a good combination, a fact I was very cognizant of as we wandered around the train depot, trying to detect Adrien's scent. We finally found it on the platform for the Macon-bound train. Boucher had been waiting here for quite some time, not too long ago.

Since the sunlight made it impossible for Michael and me to ride in the passenger cars like normal people, we stealthily slipped inside one of the freight cars which would shield us come sunrise. Michael slid the door shut and I put a keep-away spell on it as I had done to our hotel room at the Pulaski House. That should deter any overzealous inspectors from opening the doors in the middle of the day.

The train would take us to Macon and then on to Atlanta. Michael and I both agreed that Boucher would be headed north, rather than west, out of Macon. He had possession of a war god and he would want to make it to the closest battlefield he could find with all due haste.

"It'll be the middle of the afternoon when we arrive in Macon," Michael said. "However, since we don't have to change trains the sunlight shouldn't be an issue."

I looked around the freight car. "Assuming it's not riddled with holes," I muttered as I hopped up to sit on the edge of one of the wooden crates.

"We've been in worse situations, *mo ghraidh*."

"I know. I just don't relish spending the entire day dodging shafts of light."

Michael had purchased a map and a newspaper at the depot and he spread both out next to me. "We should put into Atlanta shortly after midnight," he said, pointing to the city on the map. "I think we should spend the day at a hotel there and start again after dark."

"Do you think it's prudent to waste that much time?" I asked.

"I think we'll either end up waiting in Atlanta or in Corinth," he replied.

"Is that where we're going?"

"According to the newspapers there is a large contingent of Union and Confederate forces facing off in Tennessee, just north of Corinth, Mississippi," he said, showing me the location on the map. "I believe that's where Boucher will take Ares. If I've calculated the travel time correctly, we'll arrive in Corinth on Wednesday morning if we travel straight through. I'd much rather break our journey in Atlanta. For one thing, it's a far larger city and it'll be easier to feed there."

"And if we leave Atlanta tomorrow night instead of this morning, we can take a passenger car to Dalton or Chattanooga and then hop another freight car to Corinth."

He nodded. "Where we will arrive in the early evening, instead of the early morning."

"All right," I agreed. "That is a much better plan."

"Now, the only thing left to decide," Michael said in a tone that I'd come to know all too well over the decades, "is what to do with the next fifteen hours or so?"

I narrowed my eyes at him. "I'm still angry with you."

He shrugged and grinned at me. "I like it a little rough on occasion."

I bit the inside of my cheek to keep from smiling. Even though he frustrated me at times, I loved this man more than my own life. I knew that, whatever his faults, he had only my best interests at heart. It was the black magic, not me, that he didn't trust. But the magic was a part of me and he and I were going to have to learn to live with it. If we didn't, it was going to destroy us. However, now seemed neither the time nor the place to have that discussion, especially not when his blue eyes were glittering with wickedness and his sensual lips were curved in that tempting smile I loved so well.

"Ah, lass," he coaxed. "What else have we got to do?"

I cocked one eyebrow. "So you want it rough, do you?" I asked, reaching out and grabbing a fistful of his dark blond hair. I pulled his lips to mine. "All right," I said in a soft and deadly tone. "Just try to keep up."

CHAPTER 39

It was raining when we arrived in Corinth, and had been for some time. The ground was a quagmire beneath my feet and the hem of my hooded cloak, which served to cover the beacon of my scarlet hair, was soon sodden with mud. As a result, it took us longer than I would have liked to cover the twenty or so miles north to the battlefield. There was no mistaking it when we reached our destination, though.

The sharp tang of gunpowder still permeated the air and the smell of blood and death hung all around us, a cloying scent filling my nostrils. The dark magic stirred within me, but this time it was easy to push back. As a vampire, I should have found the smell of so much blood intoxicating, but I could only think with disgust of the tragedy of so many lost lives.

"Careful," Michael whispered, pulling me up short

before I walked headlong into a group of soldiers on patrol.

The flash of Confederate gray uniforms through the trees at least signified that we were on the correct side of the lines, though how we were to find Adrien Boucher amid fifty thousand Confederate troops was beyond me. We'd verified in Atlanta that Boucher had boarded a train bound for Chattanooga, but it was strictly guesswork that he'd ended up here. A location spell would have been helpful on more than one occasion over the past three days, but to cast it required possessing an item that belonged to Adrien. It was something I should have thought of before we left the island but my head had been too wrapped up in other concerns, a fact that I was kicking myself for right now.

Michael grabbed my hand and we silently skirted a stand of what appeared to be blackberry bushes in order to avoid the soldiers.

"How are we going to find him amid all this, Michael?" I asked, detangling my cloak from the bush's thorny branches.

"We keep moving, quickly and quietly, until we pick up his scent," he replied. "I think we can skip the more densely populated camps and search only in the outlying areas. Boucher will want his privacy."

I shook my head. "It's glory he wants."

"That will come later," Michael reasoned. "Right

now he can't risk anyone seeing Ares pop in or out of that urn."

We had travelled a couple miles, slipping from shadow to shadow, when we came across something I had not expected to find—two vampires feeding on a fallen soldier. The woman stood when she sensed our arrival, but the man continued to feed. I heard the soldier moan and I started forward.

"No, Cin," Michael whispered, grabbing my wrist. "This is no concern of The Righteous."

"But they're killing that boy," I argued.

Michael pursed his lips and sadly shook his head. "They're scavengers. They feed on the dying in places such as this. The boy is dead already. They're simply putting him out of his misery."

I turned back, noticing now what I had not before. The young man had several bloody marks on his uniform, apparently bullet holes. He might have lived had those been his only wounds, but his legs had been ripped apart by cannon fire. At best a field surgeon would amputate both legs and hope he lived. But I was a vampire and I knew exactly how much blood one could lose before dying. Michael was right: the boy could not live, not with those wounds. I looked back at the woman and nodded slowly. She inclined her head to me and an understanding passed between us. This was mercy, not murder. It was a distinction I knew all too well.

"Let's go," I said, turning back to Michael. "I grow weary of this place."

The rain had finally let up and I promised myself that the first thing I was going to do when we got back to civilization was have a hot bath. It took another hour of slogging through the mud to find Adrien and Ares, but find them we did. While Claire was fighting for her life back at Kenneway, the man who professed to love her was sitting around a rebel campfire, swilling ale with the bastard who had poisoned her! I was so furious I could have happily sucked the life out of both of them on the spot.

"Well, isn't this cozy?" I announced loudly as we walked out of the shadows.

Adrien's eyes widened and he leaped to his feet, grabbing the urn and clutching it to his chest.

"Ares, kill them!" he commanded.

The war god, now clothed in a Confederate uniform, looked up at us. "I would not harm Claire's kin," he replied.

"I'm giving you an order," Boucher barked. "Kill them!"

Ares rose to his feet, looking down his patrician nose at Boucher. "You may control the urn, but I am Ares, god of war. You do not control *me*. Never forget that."

Adrien's panicked gaze darted from Ares to Michael to me. I smiled and Adrien ran, sprinting away through the woods like the devil himself was chasing him.

"Go after him," I said to Michael. "If he escapes with that urn then all this has been for nothing."

My husband laughed. "Give me five minutes and we'll be on our way."

I turned to Ares. "You have some nerve," I spat. "Do you even care what Claire is going through right now?"

Ares gave me an arrogant look. "It was a good day at war," he replied. "Claire will understand."

"You imbecile," I said with a shove to his very muscular chest. "Did you stop to think for just one minute that Claire would have never given up control of that urn willingly? Especially to the man who had kidnapped her? Or were you too busy playing the great god of war to give a thought for the woman you claim to love?"

Ares narrowed his eyes. "You are angry and scared. What has happened to Claire?"

"I don't know," I shouted. "That man you were so happily drinking with a few moments ago poisoned her to get to you. I should be there with her now but, no, I've just spent the last three days traveling across four states to get you back."

Ares grabbed me by my shoulders and shook me until my teeth rattled. "What do you mean Claire was poisoned? Is she—"

My anger vanished at the look of torment in his eyes. I sighed. "I don't know. When we left, Pandora said that the drug could kill her, but she's strong and I have every hope that she'll pull through. You should be prepared for the fact that she'll most likely lose the baby, though."

"We must return to her," he demanded. "Now."

Michael came rushing out of the woods, a small trickle of blood coming from his lip and Ares's urn held triumphantly in one hand.

"I got it!" he exclaimed.

I turned back to the war god.

"Now that Michael has the urn we can return to Corinth and catch a train—"

"There is no time for such foolishness," Ares growled.

With one hand he grabbed my arm and with the other he latched onto Michael. There was a blinding flash of light and I screamed in pain. Wind rushed over me at such a great speed that it felt as though I were caught in a cyclone. Everything went black and I was very certain that my guts would be jerked from my body at any moment. When the wind finally stopped, I fell to my hands and knees and tried not to throw up. I could hear Michael moan somewhere off to my left and I opened my eyes to try to get my bearings. What I saw before me was not the woods of Pittsburgh Landing, Tennessee. It was Claire's bedroom and the god of war was perched on the edge of her bed, holding her in his arms as she smiled over his shoulder at Michael and me.

I turned to Michael, who was lying on his back next to me, blinking up at the ceiling.

"I thought you told me he'd lost the ability to shift through time and space," Michael said.

"He had. But I do believe he's just met one of the conditions of his release," I said, smiling up at Claire, safe and sound in the arms of her lover. "He finally found something he loves more than war."

CHAPTER 40

I lay back in the tub, content in Michael's arms. Kenneway's bathroom had running water, though it wasn't heated. I didn't care. It felt entirely too good to be clean again. I let out a sigh, enjoying the cool feel of the water around us.

Claire had recovered with no lingering effects from the drug, and the baby was fine. She'd been shocked to hear that we had been concerned that she would lose the child. Claire had known instinctively what the rest of us had overlooked in our worrying—that her baby was the child of a god and nothing as mundane as a human poison would harm it. Boucher had been fortunate in that regard.

"When you took the urn back, you didn't kill him, did you?" I asked softly.

"You know I didn't," Michael replied.

No, Michael's honor would not allow him to do such a

thing. Perhaps it was a good thing that I had not been the one to go after Adrien. My morals might not have held up as well. I respected our laws but there were times when the High King's mandates were bloody inconvenient.

"He'll be back, you know," I pointed out.

"It'll take him at least three or four days to get back here," Michael replied. "We'll likely be gone by then and Claire and Ares will be safe."

"What about everyone else on the island? I have to think of them too, you know."

Michael chuckled. "I think Lizzie's proven she can take care of her own. Once Adrien knows Claire and the urn are back in Scotland, he'll have no choice but to give up. There's no way he'll ever get into Glen Gregor, after all."

I thought Michael was giving Boucher entirely too much credit. I didn't believe any of them would be safe, not while he lived.

"About that," I said. "There's something I need to tell you."

I explained to him about my conversation with Evangeline and the prospect that Claire might not be returning to Scotland after all.

"I haven't talked it over with her yet, but I think that if she wants to stay, I should let her. Even though I promised Raina I would bring her home."

Michael was quiet for a long time, thinking through the ramifications of what I'd just told him.

"You want to kill Boucher," he said flatly.

"Actually, I rather thought I'd let Ares do it," I replied.

I could feel his body relax beneath mine. Michael had never killed a human but I had a dozen deaths to my credit. I knew he didn't approve of taking a life, even Adrien Boucher's, but he was nothing if not practical and I think he knew, deep down, that this was the way it would end.

"My love," Michael said, "you know that when Devlin and Justine come, we have to leave with them. Every day the blockade tightens and we can't risk getting stuck here for the duration of the war. That could take years. If they haven't come for us in four days, though, I'll take Ares into Savannah and we'll hunt for Boucher. I can't guarantee he'll come back here, but I think it's more likely than not. But if we don't find Boucher by the time the ship comes . . . whether she wants to stay or not, she'll have to return with us, for her own safety."

I was about to agree with him when the bathroom door burst open. I rose swiftly to my knees and whirled around. Ares strode into the room, still wearing his Confederate uniform—or at least most of it. His gaze raked over me appreciatively before he turned his full attention to Michael. A little belatedly I snatched my dressing gown from the nearby chair, trying to cover myself as much as possible.

"I wish to kill this man who hurt Claire," Ares said. "Now."

Michael smiled up at me and shook his head.

"Would you get him out of here?" I hissed.

Michael rose from the tub and proceeded to shrug into his own robe. "Well, my friend, we can't do that *right* now," he explained. "For one thing, Boucher is in Tennessee. For another, you can't be far from that urn, which means that I would have to pop back there with you and I have absolutely no intention of ever repeating that experience. And even if I did, you've been free for hours now and there's a good chance of you getting sucked back into that thing and leaving me stranded God only knows where. However, Cin and I have come up with a plan I think you'll like."

As Michael tried to usher him out the door with the promise of explaining said plan, Ares clapped him on the shoulder. "Very nice, my friend," he whispered with a nod in my direction. "Are all the women in this family as wonderfully put together as ours?"

"Out!" I shouted, and a very wet sponge hit the wall not two inches from his head.

CHAPTER 41

The next night Michael insisted on taking me and Claire into Savannah.

"We'll stay at the Pulaski House again," he said. "We can drink our fill tonight and tomorrow night. During the day tomorrow we'll talk to an attorney about our plans and see about purchasing the new seeds Lizzie needs."

Though I didn't feel that feeding was a necessity quite yet, Michael was correct—it was wiser to do so now. For one thing, there was no possibility of running into Boucher in Savannah at the moment. Michael and I had talked over his plan to take Ares hunting for Boucher, and in the end we'd both decided it would be much better if Adrien came to us. Well, perhaps not better, but there would certainly be fewer witnesses.

Not to mention we're now experts at taking a body out to sea and sinking it, I thought grimly.

So in order to avoid having to leave the island to feed when Boucher's arrival was imminent, we made the trip now. Getting back into Savannah was still simple enough. Then again, we were traveling in little more than a fishing boat and hugging the coastline. I wasn't sure it would be such an easy task for a large ship coming from the open sea. I worried for Devlin and Justine and wished there was some way to get a message to them that we were no longer in the city. They would undoubtedly come here first, having no reason to believe that Michael and I would be staying out on Devil's Island.

During the carriage ride to the Pulaski House, Michael and I pointed out some of the sights of the city to Claire. She didn't have a vampire's keen night vision so perhaps she didn't enjoy the views as much as Michael and I did. I wished I could walk in the daylight just once more. I would have loved to see the city's brightly colored flowers with their faces happily turned to the sun.

When we arrived at the hotel Mr. Bennett seemed pleased to see us again. Probably because he'd just mentally raised the room rates after what had happened last time. His gaze moved speculatively over the three of us.

"One room, sir?" he asked hesitantly.

I looked across Michael to Claire, who glanced down at the urn she refused to let out of her sight, and then looked back at me worriedly. No, I definitely didn't want to share a room with her and Ares.

"Two rooms this time, Mr. Bennett," I replied.

"Very good, ma'am," he said, his face blushing a bit.

I thought it an odd reaction and I looked at Michael and Claire to see if either one of them had noticed it as well. And then I laughed out loud.

"What is it?" Michael asked softly, with a glance at Mr. Bennett.

"Nothing," I said, putting my hand over my mouth to stifle a giggle. "I'll tell you later."

I had come to feel a sort of motherly affection for Claire, being that I was technically almost fifty years her senior. Looking at the three of us as a stranger might, however, what I saw was my extremely handsome husband in the company of two young redheads who looked as though they could be sisters. I wondered just exactly what sort of man Mr. Bennett thought Michael was. What sort of women he thought Claire and I were didn't bear considering. At least the clerk seemed embarrassed that such a notion would cross his mind.

"Oh, and Mr. Bennett," Michael said as the man reached to get our keys, "I think we would all feel more comfortable having rooms on the top floor this time. You know, beyond throwing distance."

This made Bennett turn bright red. "Of course, sir," he stammered. "Again, you have our sincerest apologies. I assure you that nothing like that has ever happened at the Pulaski House before."

Michael nodded. "I should hope not."

"I wish you'd have let me give you your room free of charge, sir. This time at least, please allow me to do so."

"Nonsense, Mr. Bennett," Michael replied. "You and your hotel are hardly to blame for the random criminal act of some ruffian."

"Yes, of course, sir," Bennett replied. "Well, if there is anything I can do to make your stay more enjoyable—"

"Actually, I should like to speak to the best attorney in Savannah tomorrow afternoon."

"An attorney, sir?" Mr. Bennett squeaked.

"Oh, nothing to do with you or the hotel, my good man. It's of a personal nature."

"I'll be happy to make an appointment for you, sir," he assured Michael.

We all stared at him in silence.

"Or I could have Mr. Owens drop by the hotel at your convenience."

Michael smiled. "That would be lovely, Mr. Bennett. Ta-ta!" he called over his shoulder as he escorted Claire and me to the stairs.

"My good man? Ta-ta?" I said disgustedly under my breath.

"He thinks I'm a bloody English lord," Michael whispered back.

Claire laughed heartily. "You know, other than being kidnapped, getting pregnant, having a lunatic poison me, and almost dying, I'm having a marvelous time."

I glanced sideways at her. "You're an odd girl, Claire."

"I know," she said with a smile. "But I'm all right with that."

I thought about Pandora's claim that everyone had something dark inside them. I wondered what Claire's something was. This made me think again about Pandora and her theory about the black magic. If I did as she suggested, would it destroy me? Or would it finally give me peace? When I thought of the energy I'd expended over the last forty-four years, trying to bury that darkness deep inside me . . . I wondered what it would feel like to not have to do that anymore. But maybe that was too easy. Maybe the effort was the price I paid for having such great power. Still, the thought of what it would be like to be at peace, to not constantly feel like there were two people fighting to claim my soul . . . ah, it was tempting.

CHAPTER 42

Once we got settled into our rooms, Michael went out to feed and I went to speak to Claire. I knew that she had given some thought to staying on the plantation; that much was evident in the delirious ramblings she'd uttered while she was drugged. Before I spoke to the attorney the next day, though, I needed to know how serious she was about the prospect.

"Claire?" I said as she opened the door and ushered me inside. "I need to talk to you about something."

"Oh, no," she muttered.

I smiled and shook my head. "It's nothing bad."

"It can't be anything good," she said. "You've got that look on your face that my mother gets when I've done something unfortunate."

"You haven't done anything wrong," I assured her. "It's just that I don't really know how to put this delicately."

"Good Lord, Cin, do you really still think I'm the sort of girl you need to put things delicately to?"

I laughed. "I guess not. All right then, here it is. I promised your mother I'd bring you home, but if that's not what *you* want, I'm willing to break that promise. You know better than I do what your life at Glen Gregor is like, and what it will be like when your child comes. If that's not something you're looking forward to and you'd rather stay at Kenneway, then I'm sure Lizzie would be happy to have the company. Goddess knows Evangeline would be ecstatic."

"I can't say I haven't thought about it," she replied softly. "But what would my parents say?"

"I doubt either one of them will be very happy, but they'll come to understand in time. I'll go back to Inverness and explain everything to Raina personally and you can write them both a long letter. When the war is over I'm sure they'd be happy to come visit you. I've been in Glen Gregor in the winter and I'll wager they'd both jump at the chance to spend the season in a tropical paradise."

"You would do that for me?" she asked hopefully.

"Of course I would," I replied. "But you understand that this is all subject to us being able to eliminate the threat from Boucher. I can't let you stay otherwise." Her eyes darted to the urn and I knew what she was thinking. "I have no fear for your safety when he's around but, let's face facts, he isn't always around."

"I know," she said rather wistfully.

"And, Claire, even if he does one day break the curse . . . I've had dealings with the gods before. They aren't exactly steadfast and reliable."

"You know he can hear you," she whispered.

"Yes, well, I'm sure he knows that I speak the truth, even if he might not want to admit it," I said loudly in his direction.

Claire smiled sadly. "I'm not a fool. I know what he is. He'll probably break my heart and I don't see how this can help but end badly . . . but I love him. I want him and I'm going to take what I want for as long as I can get it. If that's foolish of me—"

"No," I said, for I knew exactly what she was feeling. After all, I'd been only a year older than she when I'd fallen in love with Michael. "No, it's not foolish. You follow your heart, Claire, and don't let me or anyone else tell you differently. Besides, you never know how things are going to turn out."

Our stay in Savannah went quickly and efficiently, with none of the excitement that surrounded our last visit, for which all of us—especially the employees of the Pulaski House—were very grateful. Against my better judgment I allowed Ares to take Claire for a stroll through the city the next afternoon while Michael and I conducted our business. I was afraid of her being left alone if he suddenly disappeared but

I wanted her to be able to see the sights in the daylight, as I could not.

Mr. Owens, the attorney, arrived promptly at one o'clock. He drew up a document for me giving Mrs. Claire Macgregor Mahone Gordon and/or Mrs. Elizabeth McCready power of attorney and the authority to act as my agent in any legal or financial matters as regarded my property in Georgia. We then spoke to a lovely young man from the City Market, ordering what seeds could still be purchased in a time of war, and arranging to have them delivered to the island the next day. It's amazing what you can manage to do from the comforts of a hotel room if you throw enough money at people. It was a productive day but by sunset I was ready to feed and go back to Kenneway.

Unlike the previous night, this evening we thought we would save time by taking Claire with us. As we left the Pulaski House, Ares's urn deposited securely in the hotel safe, I tried to explain to Claire what we were going to do and what she might see, so that she didn't get frightened. As an example I told her about the man I had fed from on my first night in Savannah.

She surprised me by asking, "Can I be the bait this time?"

"No," Michael and I said in unison.

"Why not? You'll both be there to protect me," she argued.

"Because," I said, "knowing your luck something will

go wrong and you'll get hurt. Besides, no one is going
to be the bait tonight."

Though it wasn't my usual taste in hunting, it's an
easy enough thing for a pretty woman to cast her eyes
beckoningly upon a man and have him follow her. There
was no thrill in such a feeding but it was safe and convenient, only requiring a few feet of quiet space unlit
by the city's gas lights. As for Michael's meal, only a
few blocks from our plush hotel was the waterfront and
with that came taverns and brothels. After we passed
Bay Street he had his choice among many such estab-
lishments.

"I can't believe that's really a brothel," Claire said,
looking up at the house Michael had just entered.

"Trust me," I replied. "It's not nearly as interesting
as your imagination might make it seem."

What was interesting, though, was the vampire who
followed Michael out fifteen minutes later. He was tall
and blond with a scar running down one cheek from
the outer corner of his eye to the edge of his lip. Vampires heal without leaving scars so he'd had it when he
was human. It gave him a dangerous look that I didn't
like.

"Did you notice him?" I asked Michael when he
joined us.

"Yes," he said as he took Claire's arm and we began to
walk back toward the hotel at a brisk pace. "He watched
me go upstairs and I'm assuming he's behind us now."

I was beginning to regret my and Claire's choices of gowns tonight. There was no way we were going to give a vampire the slip with Claire wearing pink and me in pale yellow. In our voluminous skirts we looked like two brightly colored flowers on either side of Michael, which was probably why he didn't even attempt to lose the vampire. He was hoping, I knew, that the public street would keep the vamp from confronting us.

"What does he want?" Claire asked.

"Who knows," I said. "He's probably not happy about strange vampires poaching on his preserves."

Claire craned her neck around. "I don't see him."

"You won't," I assured her, "Not until he's—"

"Right in front of us," Michael finished.

The vampire was lounging against a light pole, arms crossed. He was young, I could sense that, and he was cocky.

"I thought I'd sampled every beautiful neck in this city," he drawled, his eyes on Claire. "But I reckon I missed one. What do you say you two share the bounty, and I won't tell my master you're hunting in his territory?"

"That won't be happening," Michael said flatly.

The vamp pushed away from the light pole and walked to us. "You really don't want to anger him. He's got a lot more years on him than you two do."

"You're just a babe," Michael said. "You have no idea who we are."

Apparently Michael's condescending tone didn't sit well with him. Before Claire knew what was happening the vampire had snaked one hand out and grabbed her wrist. Michael went for the boy's throat and the three of them ended up in a pile on the sidewalk. Claire was shouting for me and Michael and the vampire were snarling, neither one of them willing to let go of her. I stepped forward and calmly reached into the tangle of bodies, coming up with the hand that had hold of Claire's wrist. The bone snapped and Claire struggled free, gaining her feet more quickly than I thought was possible for a human woman in hoop skirts. She rushed to stand behind me and Michael, seeing that she was free, rolled away from the vampire. By the time he stood up I had the boy by the throat.

Perhaps it was because my black magic had been such an issue lately, or perhaps it was just the over-poweringly primal instinct of a mother guarding her young, but I felt the magic stir. I let it flow through me for a brief moment, pushing it back before Claire or Michael noticed. But in those few seconds my brown eyes turned black and a look of stark terror crossed the young vampire's face.

"What the hell is she?" he shrieked, more afraid of me than the fact that Michael now had one arm clenched around his neck.

Michael laughed. "If your master is as old as you say he is, you go back to him and tell him that The Righteous let you live tonight. He'll explain to you how very lucky you are." Michael turned him loose and the boy ran. "Puppies," my husband muttered with a shake of his head.

"That was amazing," Claire said breathlessly. "Did you see how fast he ran away?"

She laughed heartily and I turned to her, shaking my head. "I do believe you mother was right when she said that trouble follows you. Let's just try to return to the hotel, collect our bags, and get back to the boat without incident, shall we?"

At least that plan went smoothly enough.

CHAPTER 43

The next afternoon was busy and, of course, Michael and I missed most of it. Occasionally Claire would pop in and give us an update on the day's events, though she quickly learned to knock first. Late in the afternoon a barge had sailed across the inlet from the mainland to deliver our seed. This method of getting from Savannah to the plantation was easier for humans, but not for vampires. While a short boat ride from the island to the coast would mean we didn't run the risk of encountering any Union gunboats, the subsequent journey to the city by carriage or wagon would have taken us all night. When you're racing the dawn, as vampires did, it was wiser to go by boat and take your chances with the patrols, at least for the time being.

Michael and I were lying in bed, listening to the voices of the men shouting back and forth to each other as they passed the house, moving the seed in wagons from the dock to the storage barns out by the fields. Lizzie had informed me that a couple of the younger men had spoken with her about going north, but that most of the slaves had families and extended families here and wanted to stay together, at least until the war ended. After that, well, I supposed we would all wait and see how the world changed for everyone on the plantation. At the moment, I was having a hard enough time keeping my own world together.

"Will you talk to me about what happened last night?" Michael asked, pulling me from my reverie. "You thought I didn't see it, but I did."

I knew Michael was talking about the fact that my eyes had turned black when I'd had that vampire by the throat. I'd been hoping that he had been too distracted to notice. I sighed, realizing that it was finally the proper time and place for us to have the conversation that had been coming for the past week.

"Michael," I said, "do you love me?"

He propped up on one elbow and looked down at me. "I think I've loved you since the day I met you," he said softly. "Why would you question that?"

"I don't," I replied, "but if you love me, then I need for you to love all of me. And I need you to trust me. Morrigan wants me to have this dark magic. I don't know why, but I have to believe she has some higher purpose than just driving me insane. The night I killed Edmund Gage and drank his blood, taking his magic inside me, Morrigan told me that I would one day be her greatest weapon. After the massacre in Edinburgh, when I asked her to cleanse the darkness from me, she refused. She said that I was now potentially everything she needed me to be. When I told her that I was not the sort of witch who practiced black magic, she said that I did not yet understand what I was."

"You never told me that," Michael said.

I shrugged. "You and Devlin and Justine, you tend to react badly if black magic is even mentioned in your presence. I suppose I felt that it was easier to keep the peace by keeping that to myself."

He brushed my hair back with his fingers. "I'm sorry if I ever made you feel that you couldn't confide in me, Cin."

"It scares you," I replied. "I understand that. It scares me too. But, Michael, my point is . . . why would Morrigan want me to have this magic if she didn't want me to *use* it?"

"I don't know," he said, shaking his head. "But Morrigan thinks only of her own plans and schemes. She's not thinking about your safety and happiness."

"I'm not sure that's fair," I said with a smile. "She gave me you, didn't she?"

He chuckled and pulled me close. I turned in his arms, snuggling against him.

"Aye, well, I'd like to think my good taste had something to do with it," he teased, then his tone grew serious once more. "I know that what Pandora offers is tempting for you. Just promise me that you'll think about this for more than a week before you decide to do anything about it."

It was more than I'd expected from him and I didn't want to worry him further by telling him that I'd already made my decision.

Instead I simply said, "I've been thinking about it for forty-four years, Michael. Eventually I'm going to have to actually *do* something, before it drives me mad."

CHAPTER 44

I had just finished dressing for the evening and was pulling my boots on when Evangeline popped up in front of me.

"Lord and Lady," I muttered. "I wish you wouldn't do that."

"Well," she said, holding her hands out, "I can't very well knock, now can I?"

"I think you're just hoping to catch my husband naked."

"Oh, I would never!" she protested, but there was a wicked smile on her face that belied her words. "Where is he, by the way?"

"Trying to summon Ares for Claire," I replied. "He's been at it without any success for about half an hour now."

"Hmm, I am in the wrong room," Evangeline muttered. "Wait a minute, I thought Claire was the only one who could summon him."

"She was until she gave the urn to Boucher. Then Michael made Boucher give it to him, therefore he now has control of it. We all decided Claire was safer if we kept it that way for now."

"She told me she was considering staying on the plantation and that you'd given her your blessing to do so," Evangeline said. "I want to thank you for that."

I waited for some impertinent comment to follow that statement, but when none did I turned to her, surprised.

"Why, Evangeline, I believe that's the first truly nice thing you've said to me," I informed her.

"At least the constant vomiting has stopped. She hasn't thrown up in days, which is nice for all of us." The ghost shrugged. "Besides, it'll give me someone to talk to about how all your 'improvements' and 'modernizations' are ruining my plantation."

I smiled. That was more like it. "I'll do my best not to bankrupt Kenneway," I assured her. "Of course, if you were really worried about that you could tell me where your father hid all his gold."

Evangeline laughed. "I think not. There isn't as much money as gossip would have you believe, but I'll be keeping that a secret until the time comes when we desperately need it."

I nodded. "Fair enough."

"Evangeline!" Claire shouted from down the hall. "Come and get your horrid beast out of my room!"

"Poor Vendetta, no one understands her but me," Evangeline said sadly, and disappeared.

"That damned feline is a menace," Michael said as he walked in the room. "Remind me of that if I ever again complain about Ravenworth's cats being too affectionate."

"Evangeline was just here. She's pleased that Claire wants to stay. She was actually civil, for the most part."

"I don't know how you stand her constant harping," Michael said.

I shrugged. "She loved a man who lied to her about everything, and then murdered her. I think she has a right to be bitter. Besides, after you learn not to take anything she says personally, she's really rather funny."

"I do admit that sometimes I feel a bit left out of the conversation around here, but all in all I think I'm glad not to be able to see her or hear her."

I put my arms around him and smiled. "Why, darling, she'd be so disappointed to hear you say that. She *likes* you."

He flushed a bit at that. "She isn't in here when we're—"

"No," I said. "Well, at least I don't think so. If she is, I can't see her."

"That doesn't make me feel better," he replied, looking around as if the ghost might suddenly appear to him.

"Is Ares finally out of the urn?" I asked.

"Yes, he is," Michael replied, "which I believe is why Claire was so eager to get Vendetta off her bed."

I laughed and wrapped my arms around my handsome husband. "Then why don't you and I take a walk?" I suggested. "We haven't had the chance to explore the whole island yet and we have at least one more day before Boucher could make it back here. Let's enjoy tonight."

And we did. We wandered through the woods, often scaring up deer, rabbits, opossums, or raccoons. On one occasion we even stumbled across two feral pigs. As we walked we tried to name the various trees we saw, some of them I only knew because I'd asked Pandora. The island boasted many oaks, cedars, junipers, palms, pines, magnolias, sweet gums, and dogwoods. It even had a small pecan grove. Every so often we would come across a mass of honeysuckle vine and I had to stop and enjoy the heavenly aroma. My honeysuckle perfume was lovely but nothing compared to the real thing.

We then left the woods and picked our way down to the beach. For a long time we sat quietly in the sand, watching the tide roll in. After that we inspected the fields and snooped through the barns and the mill where the cotton was ginned. We didn't see all of the island (I certainly had no wish to visit the salt marshes), but it was enough. Kenneway truly was one of the most beautiful places I'd ever seen.

When we finally decided to return to the house we

found ourselves to be a bit lost. The moon was nearly full, though, so at least we could gauge the general direction we needed to travel. It was a bit unnerving the way the woods tended to look the same, and several times I thought that, no matter what the moon said, we were going around in circles. Michael's sense of direction was better than mine, though, so I held my tongue and followed where he led . . . and it wasn't long before I knew exactly where we were. I could hear the drums.

Michael stopped and cocked his head to one side. "What is that?" he asked.

"Pandora and the slaves," I said. "It's some sort of voodoo. Or perhaps it's just a party. I'm not sure."

Curious as a cat, Michael followed the sound of the drums.

"This is a bad idea," I called after him.

"Oh, I'm sure they won't mind," he responded, completely misunderstanding *why* I thought it was a bad idea.

Against my better judgment, I kept silent about the magic I felt in the air and followed him. It was very late and whatever they had been doing was winding down. Four men sat around the bonfire in ladder-backed chairs, their calloused hands pounding rhythmically on the drums perched between their knees, but most of the dancers had wandered back to their cabins by now. Pandora and Ulysses were still there, though, and she looked up sharply as if she'd sensed my arrival rather

than seen it. Perhaps my magic called to hers the same
way hers called to mine. Michael shouted out a greeting and Ulysses waved back.

"Good night for a stroll," the big man said. "Gonna
rain soon, though."

I looked up at the clear night sky. The stars were
shining and there were only a few wispy clouds float-
ing across the moon.

"How can you tell?" I asked.

"I can smell it in the air," Ulysses answered, "and
feel it on the breeze."

I inhaled deeply, my sense of smell so much stronger
than his, but I didn't detect anything other than the
woods, the fire, and humans. It would be interesting to
see if he was right. Michael and Ulysses struck up a conversation about the seeds that had been delivered that
afternoon and Pandora and I wandered over to watch
the drummers. Their skill fascinated me and it was hard
to drag my eyes away from them.

"You thought any more about what I said?" she asked,
drawing my attention away from the men.

"Yes," I replied. It seemed that recently I had been
thinking of nothing *but* what she'd said. Standing in
this place of power with her, though, I hesitated. Perhaps Michael was right. Since I'd arrived on this island
my dark magic had pushed and pulled, taking me to my
limits and beyond. Suddenly it didn't appear to be the

logical time to make such a monumental decision. "I can't do it, Pandora, not now. It's too dangerous."

She snorted. "Too dangerous *not* to," she said.

"You don't know what that magic has done, what it makes me do. You don't understand—" and before I realized what she meant to do, Pandora reached down and grabbed both of my hands.

Magic arched between us and I had to struggle to keep the darkness at bay. I tried to pull away from her but it was as if the magic had hold of us both and it wouldn't let me go. Suddenly I could feel the rhythm of the drums deep inside me, pounding like the beating of a human heart, like the rapid pulse under my lips when my prey was afraid.

Pandora slid her fingers between mine, squeezing tightly. "You got to let go of that fear," she said. "Fear gives the darkness power over you. You learn not to be afraid and you'll have power over it."

"I can't," I whispered. I couldn't let go, because I *was* afraid.

"Yes, you can," Pandora insisted. "The spirits been fed well this night. They won't make mischief with your magic."

I was reminded of Raina suddenly, and the location spell we'd cast. I had held her hands and my stronger power had guided her weaker one. It made me slightly uncomfortable, and a little scared, that Pandora was now doing the same with me. I was used to my magic being stronger than any witch or wizard I faced, but solely as a practitioner of the dark arts, Pandora was far more skilled and powerful than I was. I'd never seen her use her magic and, feeling it, I didn't really want to know what sort of charms and potions she could spin with that kind of power. If I'd truly wanted to fight her I could have, and I would have won, but I was afraid I would hurt her . . . and a part of me didn't want to fight it at all.

It was at that point that Michael looked over and realized something was wrong. I could hear him yelling, arguing, threatening Pandora, but my eyes were locked on hers and I was having a hard time understanding his words. I could feel his fear, though, and my own reacted to it wildly, like cattle being caught up in a stampede.

"You got to be quiet, vampire," Pandora snapped. "Her fear's gonna drive her mad or get her killed. You want to save her, you hush now and let me set her free."

Freedom, I thought.

I closed my eyes . . . and I let go.

CHAPTER 45

I remember taking my first trip to the stables when I was a little girl. My father had held me in his arms while one of the grooms brought out a beautiful chestnut mare for his inspection. I'd been terrified of the huge animal, but my father had taken my small hand in his and together we'd stroked her sleek coat until I wasn't afraid anymore. That was, in essence, what Pandora did for me now. I let the blackness rise up, let it pour out of me until I glowed with dark light and, because of her strength, I wasn't afraid.

The darkness had always been like a terrible beast crouching inside me. I knew that it wanted blood and death, and that frightened me. My fear made me push it down, deny it sustenance until, when I did set it loose, it consumed everything in its path. Now, I felt it wash over me, through me, mingling with Pandora's own magic, pulsing with the rhythm of the drums. And suddenly everything I thought I knew seemed wrong.

Edmund Gage, the wizard who had infected me with the black magic, had been evil. That, I was not wrong about. But I was wrong about the magic. I had always been taught that all black magic was evil and, therefore, I had believed that what was inside me must be. But it wasn't. As Hamlet said, 'There is nothing either good or bad, but thinking makes it so.' Certainly, Aunt Maggie or any other witch of my line would have seen this magic's hunger for blood and death and declared it evil. But was that not what a vampire was—blood and death? Was that not what *I* was? And I was not evil.

Pandora threw her head back and laughed, enjoying the dark power rushing over us in tingling waves. Her body began to move to the beat of the drums, her hips swaying seductively. Though I wasn't sure exactly why, I held her hands and mimicked her movements, following her like a pale shadow. I closed my eyes, listened to the drums, and then I knew why she did this. I could almost hear the magic talk to me. It wanted to be fed. It wanted a purpose, to work for me as my white magic did. *You got to feed that black dog*, Pandora had said. Now I understood. I hadn't chosen it, but it was a part of me and I couldn't deny it. I had to own it, or I would never be free.

The drums beat faster and I confidently slipped my hands from Pandora's, raising my arms above my head as I danced with her. In the end, it had been such a simple thing, letting go of the fear. I knew that without Pandora I could never have done it and, by the gods, I wished I'd met her half a century ago. If I had known then what I know now, how different things might have been. Then again, maybe they had worked out exactly as they should have. Perhaps some lessons just take longer to learn.

Michael came up behind me and tentatively touched my shoulder. Slowly, I turned to him and smiled, wrapping my arms around his neck and moving my hips against his.

"Your eyes are black," he whispered worriedly, and then he shivered, feeling the magic that still surrounded me. "What is that?"

"Don't be afraid. It's darkness," I said. "And it's mine."

I turned in his arms, fitting my body flush against his, dancing in time to the drums until his manhood hardened and the rest of his body relaxed. He growled and slipped one arm around my waist, pulling me tighter, and for a long time we simply lost ourselves in the sensual rhythm of the music. We were so lost, in fact, that it took us quite a while to realize it when the music eventually stopped. I opened my eyes and looked around. The clearing was empty except for me, Michael, and the bonfire. And then it started to rain.

I tipped my head up to the sky and laughed, opening

my mouth to let the raindrops fall on my tongue. When I looked back at Michael his eyes were wild with lust. I wished I was naked in his arms, and my magic quickly made that wish a reality. When our clothes were in a sodden pile on the ground, Michael pulled me close and kissed me fiercely. His fingers bit into my thighs as he picked me up and I wrapped my legs around his waist. He carried me over and sank down in one of the chairs recently vacated by the drummers. I slid down on him, grasping the back of the chair with both hands, and leaned backward as far as I could while I rode him.

"Oh, God. Harder, lass," he growled, and I gladly obliged.

The rain poured down on us, and it felt like a thousand tiny fingers touching me everywhere. Rivulets of water ran down my breasts, cresting at the taut peaks of my nipples, then down my belly, adding to the moisture between my legs. And where the rain went, Michael's hands eagerly followed.

"I'm sorry," I gasped. "I can't wait."

I came, violently, over and over until I wanted to weep with the pleasure of it. Normally I loved to feel him come inside me, to watch his face as he found his release, but tonight I was so far gone that I simply took what I wanted.

"You were wrong," Michael said, his voice slightly shaky.

"About what?" I murmured.

"When you said coming here was a bad idea. It was a bloody excellent idea."

I smiled and kissed his neck. He had no idea how right he was.

CHAPTER 46

"We're worried," Claire's voice said, waking me from a sound sleep.

I rolled over and stretched, feeling blissfully sated and slightly sore.

"I'm fine," I assured her.

In fact, I hadn't felt this good in a very long time. As Pandora had promised, I had found the balance and my whole body was downright harmonious.

"We're not worried about you," Claire said. "Why wouldn't you be fine? We're worried about Adrien."

I opened my eyes to find Claire and Evangeline standing next to my bed, staring down at me.

"She's right," Michael said. "It's time to prepare. Depending on how quickly he's managed to travel, he could be back in Savannah today."

I looked at the clock and then glared at Claire and the ghost. I'd only been asleep for two hours.

"All right, we'll plan. But right now everyone who isn't my husband needs to get out of here and let me get dressed."

I struggled out of bed and pulled on a clean pair of breeches and a leather vest. I passed the mirror and then stopped, walked back, and looked again. Vampires might not feel the heat or the cold as humans do, but my hair certainly felt the humidity. Between that and the rolling around Michael and I had done in bed while it was drying early this morning, my normally slightly curling hair was now a riotous mass of ringlets. I ran my fingers through it but that only seemed to separate the curls and make more of them. It wouldn't have been so bad if they were all going in the same direction. Michael came up behind me, pushed the mess to one side and kissed my neck.

"How are you feeling?" he asked.

"Are you wanting to know if I feel like I might be overpowered by dark magic and suck the life out of everyone on the island? Or are you wanting to know if I'm sexually satisfied?"

"Both," he replied, looking a little embarrassed.

"I feel extraordinarily happy and content on both counts," I replied.

"Well, you certainly look like a woman who's been well-bedded," he said smugly, ruffling my curls with his fingers.

"I look like a woman who's been struck by lightning," I corrected him.

"I'll take that as a compliment," he said. "Tonight we can take a nice long bath and then I'll brush it dry for you, all right?"

"You just want to get me wet again."

He smiled wickedly. "Always, *mo ghraidh.*"

"That's not what I meant," I said, slapping his hands away. "By the way, what happened to my boots?"

"Pandora came in this morning while you were asleep and took all our wet clothes. She said she'd put the boots out in the sun to dry."

"Damn, I hope I didn't ruin them," I said.

Michael always travelled with several pairs, but I had only the one. I would have to remedy that, I decided. At the moment though, we had bigger things to worry about than my footwear. I opened the bedroom door and invited the ladies in, surprised to see that Pandora and Lizzie were also waiting. Before I could get the door closed, Vendetta slinked in and rushed across the room, hopping up onto the chaise next to Evangeline. The cat cast me a brief, triumphant look and then proceeded to ignore me and groom her tail.

"Now that we're *all* here," I said, glaring at the cat.

"Ares and I talked it over last night," Claire announced. "And he believes that the house is the most easily defendable point on the island. He said he would rather there weren't so many windows, but that at least we'd have a clear view of what was coming on all sides."

I raised my eyebrows. "Claire, darling, we're talking about one man here. He's not going to be coming with an army. He'll slip in during the day when he knows Michael and I are vulnerable and he'll probably attempt to burn the house to the ground."

"The hell he will!" Evangeline shouted.

"Now, I don't know that for sure," I said, trying to calm her. But I remembered Adrien's words: *I'll have that urn or I will burn this plantation down around you all.* "All I'm saying is that I wouldn't be surprised if he attempted it. Michael and I certainly know first-hand how fond he is of fire. Now, I've been thinking about it and I believe the plan is really quite simple. We summon Ares, the war god can have his vengeance, the island will be safe, and neither Michael nor I will have to kill Boucher and have a human's death on our conscience."

Lizzie and Pandora both looked a little uncomfortable with my plan, and I belatedly realized that I was speaking very plainly about murdering Pandora's father. I looked at her sympathetically.

"If you'd rather not be here for this, Pandora, we would all understand."

She raised her chin defiantly. "No, he's gotta get what's comin' to him. A man should be content with his lot in life, but the master always did think he was better than his raising. He wasn't nothin' but a schoolteacher's son who won my mama and Ulysses's mama and daddy in a card game. Always told me that he was too good to lay with a black woman, that my mama had put some sort of spell on him to make him come to her bed," Pandora said bitterly. "But he liked our magic well enough when it was workin' to do his bidding, like when I was feedin' all our mouths by sellin' charms and potions in New Orleans when I was fourteen. No, ma'am, he was happy enough to take that money and dress himself up so he could come out here and find some rich woman to marry. He's been reachin' above himself most of his life, lookin' for glory, and he don't care who he walks on to get it. I know he's my daddy, but the man's made his bed, now he's gotta lie in it."

I nodded. "I rather think of it this way—he tried to kill Michael and me, nearly succeeded in killing Claire, and he *did* kill Evangeline. The state would probably hang him for that. We're just saving them the trouble."

Lizzie shook her head. "He didn't murder Miss Evangeline. She fell down the stairs. Mr. Boucher said that Vendetta . . ." Claire and I were shaking our heads and Lizzie paused, and then turned to Pandora. "He didn't really push her, did he?" she asked, horrified.

The cold look on Pandora's face said it all.

"Finally!" Evangeline crowed. "Now everyone knows the truth. I can't believe that rotten bastard blamed it on Vendetta, my poor girl."

Evangeline and the cat proceeded to sympathize greatly with each other, and I turned back to Lizzie.

"All right," she said eagerly, "we let Claire's god kill him. Are you sure it's going to be that easy?"

"No," Michael said. "I think we need to prepare for the fact that Boucher is a sneaky bastard and Ares can't always come when he's summoned."

"Well, I certainly don't intend to put my fate solely in the hands of a god, I assure you," I said. "That was simply the bare bones of the plan. Now we have to work out all the details. I want to be prepared for anything. I underestimated Boucher's sneakiness before and I won't do it again."

Michael nodded. "The danger isn't so much Boucher himself, it's what he can accomplish before we even know he's on the island. Ares was right about one thing, the house does give us an advantage. The porches are wide enough that most of the direct sunlight stays out of the rooms. That makes it possible for you and me to move around the house as long as we pay attention to where the sun is. And the three hundred and sixty degree views mean that he can't torch the house from a vantage point where we can't see it."

"Ares was wrong about the windows, though," I said. "They're actually an asset. As long as I can see Boucher, I can take him out with my magic. Then we simply have to drag him in, tie him up, and deliver him to Ares."

"Doesn't seem very sporting, though, does it?" Michael pointed out.

I looked at him incredulously. "Neither was kidnapping Claire, or throwing a . . . missile through our hotel window, or—"

Michael held his hands up in surrender. "You're right," he agreed. "I will happily truss him up like a Christmas goose."

"Thank you, dear," I replied sweetly. "Now, what we need is a map of the island."

"There are several in the estate office downstairs," Evangeline said.

"I'll go get them," Claire offered.

When she returned we laid the map out on the bed. Devil's Island was an oblong stretch of land. The dock, main house, overseer's cottage, and the slave village were all located at the northern end. The fields ran down the middle of the island farther south, past the village. I pointed to the dock on the map.

"This is the problem," I said. "Even if we post a lookout, because of the shape of the island a boat isn't visible until it's nearly at the dock. What would be helpful is to have someone posted on the beach where they could see a boat coming from far away. Of course, the downside of that is that by the time said person got all the way back to the house with a warning, it would be too late."

"There are a couple of signal flares in the boat," Michael suggested. "I remember being surprised to see them."

My eyes lit up. "The only way Boucher can get on the island is from the seaward side or across from the mainland. We could post Hector on the beach and his cousin Perseus on the dock, each with a flare." I said tapping the map.

"What's to stop him from docking anywhere he pleases on the mainland side of the island?" Claire asked.

"Gators," Pandora replied. "That coast is all salt marshes. He try to sneak in that way and we won't have to worry about him 'cause the gators'll get him first."

"So we put the boys on the beach and the dock and the flares will give us ample opportunity to know he's coming," Claire said. "But don't you think we ought to find out *if* he's coming before we go to all that trouble?"

"He'll be back," Pandora said. "Man's got a powerful sense of what he believes to be his destiny. Won't go easy on him to have it taken away."

"Well, all right," Claire conceded, "but you left him in Tennessee. There are a lot of miles between there and here. He could have been impressed into the army, blown up by a cannonball on the field of battle, hit by a train . . . we don't even know if he's still alive."

"Hit by a train sounds splendid," Evangeline happily interjected.

Claire turned to me. "You did a location spell with

my mother in order to find me. All you need is a personal item. He couldn't have taken everything with him in those two bags. Surely he left something behind we could use."

"He kept his cufflinks and cravat pins in that box on the chest of drawers," Evangeline suggested.

"Thank you, Evangeline," I said, mostly to let Michael, Pandora, and Lizzie know she'd offered a helpful suggestion.

I walked over and picked up the ornately carved mahogany box. Opening it, I discovered it empty except for a single gold band. I snapped the lid shut. It would be the perfect thing to use for the spell, but I couldn't bring myself to tell Evangeline that her louse of a husband had taken his cufflinks and left his wedding ring behind.

"There's nothing in it," I lied.

"Oh! I know!" Evangeline said excitedly. "Look through all those drawers. A couple months before he killed me Adrien came back from a trip to Savannah wearing this ridiculous monocle. I told him it made him look like a pompous ass and he never wore it again. I don't know where he stashed it, but it has to be here somewhere."

I sent Claire and Evangeline back downstairs to the estate office to locate a map of the United States, or at least the South, while I conducted a quick search of the room. I uncovered several drawers full of Adrien's older clothes, which I promptly gave to Pandora to pass along to the men in the village, and one gold monocle wrapped in a handkerchief and tucked behind a book on Greek mythology in the nightstand drawer.

"I've never seen a magic spell done before," Lizzie said, wide-eyed with excitement.

"Well, let's hope it works like it's supposed to," I replied. "My spells don't always."

Claire and Evangeline shortly returned with another map. We spread it out across the bed and, just as Raina had taught me, I set the monocle on its side in a neutral spot and focused my power. I had to hold it upright with one finger until the magic took hold, then I moved my hand away and it spun by itself until I recited the incantation.

"Treacherous villain who's schemed and lied / Show me the place where you reside," I called out.

The monocle began to roll and I nearly lost my concentration when Lizzie gasped. I managed to hold it together, though, and in just a few seconds the lens dropped . . . right over Savannah.

"I guess that answers that question," I said dryly.

CHAPTER 47

Once we knew that Boucher was close, the five of us (and Evangeline, though she didn't do much but offer sarcasm) began to prepare for his eventual arrival. Pandora packed up baskets of food for Hector and Perseus and also suggested that each boy take one of his friends with him for company. The boys treated the whole thing like a grand adventure, but they also understood the gravity of the situation.

Since planting was behind schedule and Ulysses had most of the adults out in the fields all day, we engaged the island's children to help us watch the sky for flares. Under the previous management, most of the children would have also been out working in the fields, but I would not allow that. I believed that children should be children; they would have the rest of their lives to work. For the next few days, though, they all knew to keep a watchful eye to the sky.

As the day wore on into evening and no green flares burst overhead, Michael and I began to relax. I knew that Boucher wouldn't come at night. He knew what we were. When he came, it would be with the sunlight at his back. Even so, Michael and I sent everyone else to get a good night's sleep and we stayed up, sitting on the second story porch and keeping watch.

At nine o'clock the next morning a great hue and cry went up in the yard. The flare from the dock had been spotted. I rolled out of bed and Michael helped me dress as quickly as was possible considering my boots still weren't dry and I had to wear a dress. The pale gold evening gown was quite inappropriate for a Friday morning but, being a vampire, I'd never seen the point in spending money on day gowns. By the time Michael finished with the buttons, Pandora had shooed all the children back to the relative safety of the village, and Cassandra had taken Ginny and the baby back to Lizzie's cottage. I tried to get Lizzie to leave with her children but she wouldn't go.

"You might need me," she said and gave me a look that brooked no refusal.

With the area around the main house deserted except for the five of us, we gathered in the upstairs hall with the urn and waited. Pandora stood on the porch, watching the drive from the dock.

"Here come the boys," Pandora announced.

The two of them skidded to a halt in front of the house. "He's comin' from the mainland," Hector shouted up to Pandora. "An' it looks like he's got a whole army with him! Must be twenty men in that boat!"

Pandora turned to me wide-eyed.

"Tell the boys to go through the woods to the beach," I said. "And to stay there with Hector until someone comes to tell them it's safe to return to the house."

"You said he wouldn't come with an army," Claire felt the need to point out. "Why does he have all those men with him?"

"It's a lynch mob," Michael said grimly.

Damn Adrien Boucher, I thought. This meant that we would have to adjust our plans a bit. We couldn't very well turn Ares loose to smite him in front of twenty witnesses.

"What are we going to do?" I whispered to Michael. "I never thought he'd be able to talk anyone else into being a party to his vengeance."

"You're all going to stay in here and let me go out and talk to them," Lizzie said. "I know these people and if I can convince them that they're terrorizing a house full of helpless women, maybe I can shame them into going home."

We argued back and forth about the validity of that idea until the debate was halted by the sound of the rear door slamming. A moment later Ginny McCready came rushing up the stairs, blonde braids flapping behind her.

"Ginny! I told you to stay with Cassandra," Lizzie scolded.

"No, Mama," the girl protested, clutching her mother's calico skirt. "I'm staying with you."

"They're here," Pandora said. "The master and what looks like a goodly portion of what's left of Savannah's white trash."

Lizzie marched out onto the porch at the end of the hall and Michael and I moved as far forward as the sun would allow, trying to see what was going on. At any other time of day this end of the hall would have been shaded, but the morning sun shone directly on the front of the house. Claire, Pandora, and Ginny stood just inside the doors, watching as Lizzie marched up to the railing and put her hands on her hips.

"Mr. Boucher," Lizzie called down to him, "none of you have any business being on this island. What's the meaning of this?"

I hardly recognized Adrien; he looked as though he'd aged ten years since I'd last seen him. His Confederate uniform was dirty and rumpled and he had at least a week's growth of whiskers on his face. His normally impeccably combed hair was greasy and disheveled, as if he'd been tugging at it in frustration. Gone was the slick gentleman and in his place stood a man who appeared almost rabid. That was worrisome enough, but the torches and guns he and the other men carried made it doubly so.

"Lizzie," Boucher said in greeting. "Word in Savannah is that your husband's no longer Kenneway's overseer."

Of course, I thought. *The men who delivered the seed would have noticed McCready's rather conspicuous absence.*

"And what business is that of yours, Mr. Boucher?" Lizzie asked.

There was a pause and then Adrien said, "Well, none, but I'd sure like to know where he is."

"Then that makes two of us," Lizzie replied. "He's probably laid up in some whorehouse in Charleston. Or maybe Yankee gunboats got him. All I know for sure is that he left this island over a week ago and I've not seen hide nor hair of him since."

"Really?" Boucher said with a smile. "I see the island's boat is tied up at the dock. Exactly how did he leave, Lizzie? He fly away like a bird? Because me and these men are thinking that witch Cin Craven killed him and drank his blood in one of those black sabbaths Reverend Simmons is always warning us about."

Lizzie laughed. "You all know Robert McCready. Now, you tell me whether it's more likely that he was killed by a witch than it is that he just plain ran off on his wife and children."

There was some murmuring from the mob that perhaps Miss Lizzie had a point.

"When you've got some sort of proof that someone

on this island harmed my husband in any way," she added, "you come back with the proper authorities. Until then, you men should be ashamed of yourselves, coming out here and harassing innocent women and children this way. Douglas Foreman—yes, I see you back there—I know your mama raised you better than this."

"Don't listen to her," Boucher shouted to the men. "If she's really innocent, then why doesn't Cin Craven come out here and tell me that herself?"

Oh, he was just loving this, the bastard.

"I'll tell you why, because she's so evil she can't even walk in the light of day or God will strike her down," he extolled. "As good Christians, should we let something like that defile our land? Let her come out or let her burn for the witch she is. We're doing God's will here, boys. We shall not suffer a witch to live!"

"This isn't working," Evangeline hissed in my ear. "Do something before that lunatic burns down my house!"

There were rumblings from the other men, a few shouts of "amen" and a general consensus that if I wouldn't come outside, they'd be duty-bound to burn me out. It always amazed me how normal, rational people could get caught up in this sort of insanity. But humans do love a mob, and a mob is not the vampire's friend.

Visions of what had happened to witches in the Burning Times floated through my head. Men, women, and even children who had been accused of witchcraft had been horribly tortured and then drowned, hanged, or burned at the stake. I clenched my teeth, and it suddenly occurred to me that I was no longer worried . . . I was very, very angry.

"You send her out here, Lizzie, or you're not gonna like what happens next," Boucher informed her. A rousing cheer followed this which only infuriated me further.

Who did these men think they were, anyway? Other than their guns and their inflated egos, what made them think they could come onto *my* property and threaten *my* people? I was the Red Witch of The Righteous and I would not be cornered and trapped by a bunch of "white trash," as Pandora had called them.

Pandora felt it, the rise of my magic, and turned to me. Michael saw the look on her face and he grasped my hand.

"Cin," he said, "your eyes. I know you think you have control of this now but that hasn't actually been tested. We can get away with McCready disappearing, we might even be able to get away with Boucher's death, but if something goes wrong and you kill fifteen men you'll have the entire city of Savannah out here on this island with guns and torches."

"Don't worry, darling," I said confidently. "I'm not going to kill anyone. I'm just going to make very certain that no one else will ever have the guts to set foot on this island uninvited again. Lizzie," I called to her. "Tell them I'll come out, and then you get inside where it's safe."

"You can't go out there," Michael protested. "The sun! You'll burn!"

I squeezed his hand. "Have a little faith, dear."

Claire and Pandora grabbed Ginny's hands and moved quickly to stand behind Michael. When Lizzie was inside I closed my eyes and focused my energy. For the first time the black magic wasn't something entirely separate from the white. Oh, I could feel the difference. It wasn't a blending; my magic would never be gray. It was more like mixing oil and water in a jar. Eventually it would separate and the light would rise to the surface while the darkness settled back into that shadowy place deep inside me.

But at the moment I intended to shake the jar, and see what happened.

CHAPTER 48

The wind picked up, rushing with an eerie sigh down the oak-lined drive from the dock. The Spanish moss began to sway like ghosts in the tree branches and the breeze scattered fallen Magnolia leaves among the men's feet like scurrying mice. Thick black clouds rolled in from the sea, tumbling over each other in a rush to claim the sky from the sun. Soon the entire island was cloaked in darkness.

I stepped out on to the balcony in my gold tissue gown with its wide skirts, my scarlet hair spilling down my back like a fall of rubies. Contemptuously I looked down on the men below. The black magic could feel their fear, and that pleased me.

"Where the hell did this storm come from?" one whispered.

"Boucher said the sun can't touch her," said another.

"Reckon a handmaiden of Satan would really be

wearing a big ol' cross around her neck like that?" asked a third.

"Gentlemen," I said coldly. "You are trespassing."

"What did you do to Robert McCready?" someone at the back of the crowd was brave enough to shout.

"She killed him, that's what she did," Boucher announced.

"'He that is without sin among you, let him first cast a stone.' That man would not be you, Adrien," I responded. "Gentlemen, you see before you a man who murdered his wife and attempted to murder me, my husband, and my cousin. I'm not the one who should be the focus of your misguided justice."

"Can handmaidens of Satan quote the Holy Scripture?" someone whispered.

"You don't reckon he really did all that, do you?" came another voice from the crowd.

"She's a witch!" Boucher shouted. "How else do you explain how the sky turns from day to night in a matter of minutes? She must burn! It is God's will!"

"You don't give a badger's ass about God or His will, Adrien Boucher," I spat. "All you want is vengeance because I took something from you that you didn't want to give up." I placed my hands on the iron railing and leaned forward. Very slowly, so that they all understood, I said, "Gentlemen, I'll let you in on a little secret. I *am* a witch and I have claimed this island. Everyone on it is under my protection. Now, I would suggest that you all leave my property . . . *and don't ever come back.*"

"Ha! She admits it!" Adrien shouted. Then he took his torch and pitched it like a javelin at the balcony.

I held my hand up and it exploded in mid air, raining shards of wood and glowing embers down in front of the mob.

"Don't make me tell you again," I stated coldly.

With that several men turned and ran, but my little show of force only spurred the others on. A flash of gray caught my peripheral vision and I turned to see Michael vault over the railing, landing like a cat on the ground below.

"If you think you're going to burn this house down with women and children inside it," he announced loudly, "you're going to have to come through me to do it."

I heard a metal click and was surprised to see Lizzie step up next to Michael, her gun raised to her shoulder.

"And me. This rifle shoots twenty-eight rounds per minute, boys," she said confidently. "I might not get all of you, but who's going to be first?"

Oh, I wish they hadn't done that, I thought. While I trusted Michael with his fists and Lizzie with her gun, these men also had guns and fists and we were still outnumbered. Before anyone got the bright idea to be the first to step on up, I somehow had to neutralize the situation.

All right, I said to the black magic, *you wanted to come out and play, let's see what you can do.*

With my magic now working in harmony, I felt connected to everything—the clouds rolling through the sky, the wind whistling through the trees. I could even feel the dark presence of Pandora's power. Reaching further I recognized the familiar feel of Claire's small bit of magic, and the neck-ruffling necromancy she'd inherited from her father. I sensed Evangeline hovering like a nebulous shadow behind me.

Suddenly, as if the black magic had a mind and will of its own and had just come up with a brilliant idea, it rushed from me, not over the men below but east and west, disappearing into the dark woods. I could still feel it connected to me, pulling at me like sticky taffy. Whatever it was going to do it had better do it quickly because the situation on the ground was rapidly deteriorating. A very large man was about to take a swing at my husband and Lizzie was holding off several others who were unwilling to shoot at a woman. Adrien Boucher was watching me, waiting.

The sound of an army of footsteps marching across the packed earth filled my ears. The men below heard it as well and the shouting and name-calling dwindled until there was nothing but stunned silence on the ground. I walked to the far edge of the porch, hoping that it wasn't the field workers coming with some misplaced idea that they could help. But there was nothing human coming down the lane from the village. When I saw what my magic had called forth, I laughed. The darkness liked death, and death was exactly what it had brought me.

I had emptied the entire slave cemetery and the spirits were now marching on the house. The mob took one look at the ghostly army and began to slowly back away from the house. I rushed back to the center of the porch, smiling as the angry, belligerent men turned wild-eyed with fear.

"Go!" I shouted. "And don't ever come back!"

Like a cresting white wave the spirits rushed the men, swirling around them, screaming with a sound like metal scraping across glass. The humans began literally falling all over themselves in an effort to get away. From the family cemetery on the other side of the house I saw a man and woman sail forth, she in a high-necked white gown and he wearing evening clothes, bushy sideburns, and a top hat. I happily watched as Evangeline danced through the departing mob with her parents, whirling like a dervish and laughing.

As the men ran like rats abandoning a sinking ship, the sound of ghostly voices followed them, whispering in their ears, hounding their every footstep. Over and over the voices warned, "This land is mine. . . . Don't ever come back. . . . Don't ever come back. . . ."

CHAPTER 49

When their task was complete, the ghostly forms melted to the ground until they were nothing more than fog rushing across the grass, and disappeared from whence they came. All save Evangeline, who was standing triumphantly amid the scattered and smoldering remains of the men's torches. Unsurprisingly, Adrien Boucher was the only one who hadn't run, which just goes to prove that the thirst for vengeance will overcome good judgment and all sense of self-preservation.

Michael smiled at him. "You would have been wise to stay in Tennessee," he said.

"Do you understand what you did?" Boucher screeched. "We could have won that battle, a great victory for the south, and then you took him away from me. Over twenty thousand casualties on both sides, half of them ours."

"Welcome to the horrors of war, Boucher. Don't you

believe for a moment that there would have been any fewer lives lost with a blood-thirsty war god on the field. But, then, it's not the dead and wounded that you really care about, is it? You certainly got away unscathed," Michael observed contemptuously. "I'll wager you didn't even stay to fight, did you? You want to be like your heroes of myth and legend, but you don't have it in you, mate, and you never will."

"Fort Pulaski on the Savannah River fell to the Union yesterday, did you know that?" Adrien asked. "Our whole way of life is going to be stripped from us and before you know it the Negroes will be giving orders to the white men!"

"Well, wouldn't that be the end of the world," Michael said sarcastically. "I'll tell you what," he offered, "since it's obvious that you won't let this go, why don't I summon the god himself and if he wishes to go away with you to war, I'll give you the urn."

Boucher's eyes glittered at the prospect.

"Ares!" Michael shouted. "I summon you."

In a flash of light the god appeared in front of Michael. His Confederate uniform was gone and he was once again wearing his bronze armor. He looked from Michael to Boucher and smiled.

"This is the little man who hurt Claire," Ares said. "I will kill him now."

Boucher, belatedly realizing that all was lost, began to back away. He pulled his pistol from the waistband of his breeches and fired it at Ares. The bullet hit the armor and bounced off, landing harmlessly on the ground. And that's when Boucher panicked.

Ares raised one arm toward him and Adrien started firing wildly. Michael dove toward Lizzie, pushing her to the ground, trying to shield her with his body. A stray bullet caught me in the chest, just above my left breast, the force of it knocking me to the floor. Adrien kept firing until his gun clicked impotently.

The war god strode over to him, reaching out one massive hand and grabbing Boucher by the throat. Adrien clawed frantically at Ares's wrist but his efforts didn't leave so much as a scratch on the god's skin.

"Human," Ares spat, "you dared to try and take from me the only thing I've cared about for millennia, a woman who is pregnant with my child."

"It wasn't my intention to kill her," Boucher choked out.

"Cease your lies," Ares demanded. "You wanted the attention of the great god of war. Now you have it."

Ares tossed Boucher away from him and for a moment I thought he was going to let the man go. Adrien must have thought so too, for he scrambled to his feet, stumbling backward in an effort to flee. I watched through the iron railings as Ares raised one massive arm and threw a god-bolt at Boucher. Adrien's screams echoed in my ears as the blue lightning hit his chest and his whole body went up in flames, incinerating him to ashes within seconds.

Pandora told him he'd burn in God's fire for what he'd done, I thought. *She just had the wrong god.*

I sighed gratefully. It was finally over.

"Oh, God!" Pandora screamed from inside the house. "Help! Come quick! Oh, God . . . Miss Claire!"

Ares flashed into the hall just as I burst through the doors. For a moment we both stood like statues, shocked by the scene before us. Claire was sprawled on the floor in Pandora's arms, clutching her stomach just below her breasts . . . and blood was seeping out from between her fingers at an alarming rate. I rushed forward, sliding to the ground in front of her.

"Oh, Claire," I breathed. This was bad.

"Stray bullet," she said raggedly. "Curiosity killed the cat." She started to laugh but stopped, a pained expression on her face. "Damned cat's fine though . . . and I'm going to die."

"You're not going to die," I lied, peeling her fingers away from the wound. The situation did not get better upon closer inspection.

No, I thought. *I lost Fiona and I lost Archie. I can't lose Claire too. Not now.*

Michael and Lizzie rushed up the stairs, coming to an abrupt halt behind Ares, expressions of fear on both their faces.

Claire looked up at the war god, tears gathering in her

eyes. "I'm so sorry about the baby," she said. "I wanted to be the mother of your child so much, truly I did."

"You can save her," Pandora said desperately. "Make her a vampire. Do it now!"

She would lose the baby and she would never be able to have another, I thought, *but she would live.*

"No," Ares said harshly, as if he could read my thoughts. "She will not be one of Morrigan's creatures. She is mine!"

With that he shoved Pandora away, scooped Claire into his arms, and disappeared in a violent flash of light. We were all left staring at the empty, blood-stained space Claire had just occupied.

"Where did he take her?" Evangeline asked.

I shook my head. "I don't know," I replied, and then staggered into the wall.

I looked down and for a moment I couldn't figure out why the front of my gown was red with blood. I'd forgotten about the bullet in my chest.

"Damn," I muttered.

CHAPTER 50

Ginny McCready, who had thankfully been hiding under the covers on my bed during most of the confrontation, now sat next to me with a fascinated look on her face as Pandora dug the bullet out of my chest.

"Doesn't it hurt?" she asked.

"A bit," I replied nonchalantly.

Actually, it burned like fire, but I wasn't going to tell her that. Lizzie didn't have quite the stomach for blood and gore that her daughter did, so she'd promptly left and gone down to the cottage to tell Cassandra to inform the others that the threat was gone. I glanced down again at the wound and my lovely dress that was now completely ruined. Michael tipped my chin up and kissed me on the lips.

"You were incredible," he said softly.

"You weren't so bad yourself," I replied. "But next

time let's try not to openly challenge a mob of fanatics carrying guns, shall we?"

"I was just distracting them so you could do what you do best," he said with a grin.

Lizzie entered the room just as Pandora pulled the bullet out. Ginny whooped with delight at a mission accomplished and I sank back onto the pillows, feeling utterly drained.

"I'm beginning to hate guns," I complained. "Swords make so much cleaner wounds. Do you realize this is the second time I've been shot in the past year?" I cracked one eye open. "Lizzie, when I'm stronger I want you to teach me how to use that rifle," I said.

"How long will it take you to recover?" Lizzie asked. "I sort of thought you vam—" she broke off, looking at Ginny, who was soaking everything up like a sponge.

"Mama, I know she's a vampire," Ginny stated. "Pandora already told me."

We all looked at Pandora in shock. She shrugged. "Child asked," she said. "Wasn't gonna lie to her."

Lizzie grimaced. "Yes, well, when she asks you how babies are made I'd appreciate it if you'd lie," she said under her breath.

"I know that too," Ginny informed us.

"That's enough, young lady," her mother scolded.

I coughed and answered Lizzie's question. "It'll heal faster after I've fed."

Michael shook his head. "If Boucher was right and

Fort Pulaski has fallen to the Union, it'll be nearly impossible to get into Savannah anymore. We'll have to go across the inlet to the mainland tonight and hope to find something there."

"Take mine," Lizzie offered.

I shook my head. "Lizzie, you don't—"

"Cin," Michael interrupted. "If she's willing, let her do it. You're wounded and there's no telling what we're going to find. I'll have to go, but finding one meal is a lot easier than finding two."

"Ain't no reason you can't take my blood, is there?" Pandora volunteered. "She's scared of my magic but you ain't got a lick of magic in you, sir. Take it with my blessing," she said, holding out her wrist to him. "As penance for betrayin' Miss Claire."

"You don't owe me that," Michael said.

"Mr. Michael, you won't take it from me, then take it from one of the others," Pandora argued. "You gave them the hope of freedom. Any one of them'd be happy to spill their blood for you."

Michael accepted Pandora's offer of blood and Lizzie sent Ginny out into the hall, firmly closing the door behind her. When Lizzie turned back to me she had a worried expression on her face.

"Is it going to be like what you did to Robert?" she asked. "I don't mind, I just want to be prepared."

"No," I said. "It won't be anything like that."

I explained the process to her and Pandora and then

Michael and I bespelled them both and drank gently from their wrists. At one point I glanced up to see Ginny peeking in from the hall. I made a shooing motion with my hand and she grinned and softly closed the door. Just as we'd finished, the sound of heavy footsteps climbing the stairs reverberated through the house. Ulysses pushed open the bedroom door and breathed a sigh of relief to see his wife unscathed.

"We was down in the far field when I saw the flare," he said. "Everyone all right?"

"Miss Cin was wounded but she'll be fine," Pandora informed him.

He glanced around the room, mentally counting heads. "Where's Miss Claire?" he asked.

Yes, I thought, *that's the question, isn't it?*

CHAPTER 51

We tried to summon Ares. We shook the urn and tried again. Nothing happened. Growling in frustration I threw the thing against a wall but, as Claire had said, it was absolutely indestructible.

"We'll wait for twenty-four hours and try again," Michael said.

"I don't want to wait," I snapped petulantly. "I want to know what's happened to her now."

He wrapped his arms around me. "I know," he said. "But I think she's safe. Ares wouldn't have taken her away just to watch her die."

"He might have if he thought I was going to make her a vampire," I replied.

Michael shook his head. "He's a man in love. He'd rather have her a vampire than dead. Trust me, I know this."

I smiled up at him sadly. "You do, don't you?" After all, he had turned me to save me.

The rest of the day was agonizingly long. Michael tried to distract me but I paced until Evangeline complained good-naturedly that I was going to wear a hole in her hardwood floors. Actually, the ghost was just as worried for Claire as I was. In fact, the entire household was quiet and subdued, the only sounds coming from the children outside.

Hector and Perseus were hailed as heroes. When they returned from the beach, all the children gathered around to hear the story of how Perseus had lit the flare and then they wanted to hear from Hector what it was like to pilot the boat. Ginny had joined in, telling everyone about what had happened at the house. I'm not sure how much of this she actually saw and how much she'd heard from Pandora. Some of it she definitely made up, but she told it with flair anyway. To hear her tell it, you'd think I had single-handedly slain an eight-headed hydra instead of simply scaring off a handful of overzealous wastrels with a bit of magic.

At dusk Lizzie marched into my room, rifle in hand.

"Come on," she said. "I'm going to teach you how to shoot."

I started to protest, but Michael stopped me.

"Go ahead, lass," he said. "It'll take your mind off of it. We can't do anything until in the morning anyway."

Lizzie took me out into the woods and tacked a piece of red cloth to a tree. Then she showed me how to load and fire the rifle. The first shot I missed entirely, the second one hit dead center on the target. Lizzie congratulated me and I felt a silly sense of pride at being able to hit what I was aiming at. After that, I realized that shooting was a wonderful way to vent my anger. I used up a whole box of ammunition and Lizzie was amazed to find that I was accurate to about four hundred yards. Of course, as I pointed out to her, it's very helpful to your aim if you're a vampire who can *see* four hundred yards away in the dark. As we walked back to the house I thought that perhaps I didn't hate guns after all. I just hated being shot.

Eventually I slept, though I was grateful when Michael woke me and told me it was time. Dressing quickly in my breeches, a white shirt, and the leather vest, I was happy to see that Pandora had returned my dry boots. Promptly at ten o'clock Lizzie, Pandora, and Evangeline arrived, all of them eager to see if we could finally get Ares out of that urn and find out what had happened to Claire. Michael said the words to summon him and we all waited breathlessly (some of us more than others) to see if he would appear.

"You are the neediest bunch of people I've ever met," Ares said as he flashed into the room. "I haven't been home in three millennia and I can't even enjoy it because your calls echo constantly through my temple.

Claire insists that I must come down here and tell you that she's fine. So here I am."

I clutched Michael's hand in relief. "Where is she?" I asked. "What did you do with her?"

"What about the wound?" Pandora demanded. "Is she really all right?"

"I just said she was, did I not?" he asked impatiently. "She's in my temple on Mount Olympus and she is healed."

"How?" I asked.

Ares looked a bit uncomfortable but when I repeated the question he answered. "I took her to Athena and offered to spend the rest of eternity trapped in that urn if she would intercede with Asclepius to save Claire and my child."

"If Claire is healed," Michael said suspiciously, "then how did you get out?"

"Because the curse is broken," I said. "He finally loved something else more than he loved war or himself."

Ares nodded. "Claire was given ambrosia and now she will never die. She will stay with me always on Olympus."

"We won't ever see her again?" Evangeline asked sadly.

"I will bring her to visit after our child is born," Ares assured her.

I narrowed my eyes. "If Claire is truly healed, why didn't she come to tell us herself?"

"She refuses to travel until after the birth," he replied. "She says shifting hurts worse than being shot."

"I can vouch for that," Michael muttered.

Ares shrugged. "I told her it won't feel the same now that she's had ambrosia, but she insists upon worrying about the child."

"If she won't come here, then you can take me to her," I stated. "I won't go back to Inverness and lie to her mother. I want to see for myself that Claire is all right and that she's happy."

"I can't take you to Olympus," Ares scoffed.

"Why not?" I asked.

"Because it isn't done," he replied. "It's completely against the rules."

Since when does he care about rules? I thought. Well, probably since he's spent the last several thousand years trapped in a jar. I suppose that would certainly adjust anyone's attitude. Still, that was hardly my concern.

I walked up to him, hands on my hips. "That isn't a good enough answer."

He glared down at me. "You will not force my hand on this, vampire. I have given you the word of a god that your cousin is unharmed. That should be all you require."

I jerked my head back at his arrogance. "Ares, if you don't take me to her, I'll—"

"You'll what?" he interrupted. "I am a god, you

cannot hurt me. You cannot kill me. Exactly what leverage do you think you have?"

"Do not ever tell me that I can't do something," I said, looking him straight in the eye. "If you don't let me see Claire, I promise you that I will spend the rest of my unnaturally long life finding ways to make you miserable."

"You can try," he said smugly, and disappeared.

We were all silent for a moment and then the room erupted into curses and questions.

"That son of a bitch!" I shouted.

"Miss Claire ain't gonna like that at all," Pandora said ominously.

"Do you really think he'll bring her and the baby back here?" Lizzie asked.

"I think he's a liar," Evangeline spat.

"I should have tossed that damned urn in the ocean the first night we were here," Michael said.

This went on for several minutes until Ares quite unexpectedly flashed back into the room. He glared at me and grabbed my wrist. Michael shouted a warning and reached for his sword.

"Sheath your weapon, my friend," Ares said with a weary sigh. "Apparently I must do as the vampire requests or I'll never sleep with my wife again."

I smiled triumphantly at him. Good for Claire!

"You have two minutes," he warned me. "And if you ever tell anyone I did this . . ."

CHAPTER 52

Having experienced shifting, as Ares called it, I could readily and wholeheartedly agree with Claire's reluctance to do it again. It didn't get any better upon a second try.

"That's bloody awful!" I said, mortified that Ares had to hold me up so that I didn't end up sprawled on the marble floor.

"I suppose it takes some practice," he said. "Which you will not be getting."

"Cin!" Claire's chipper voice shouted and a moment later she nearly knocked me over as she hugged me fiercely.

I wrapped my arms around her. "You are alive," I said happily. "Let me look at you."

She was dressed in a flowing white gown with her red hair pulled back and fastened with diamond pins.

She twirled around for my inspection, looking positively radiant.

"I can't believe you got shot," I said rather bluntly.

Claire laughed. "Of course you can."

Well, that I would have to concede. It was poetic justice, though, that the unluckiest girl I'd ever known had ended up an immortal with a Greek god in her bed.

"Evangeline still thinks I should have made you a vampire," I told her. "She misses you. We all do."

Claire smiled. "And I miss you. Tell Evangeline that I'll come visit and bring a passel of children who will be able to see her and talk to her. And tell my parents that I will see them too, and that everything worked out the way it was supposed to. Ares knew how desperately I wanted to be a mother and he offered to sacrifice himself to give me that opportunity."

"And that gesture not only saved you, but freed him from his prison," I stated.

She smiled and nodded.

"Are you happy, Claire?" I asked.

"I didn't know one person could be this happy, Cin," she said. "And you should see the temple. It's beautiful!"

I looked skeptically at the austere, unrelieved white marble in the massive throne room.

"Oh, it's not all as somber as this," she assured me. "The rest of it is quite lovely and the gardens are spectacular."

"Perhaps some satin cushions would cheer things up a bit," I suggested with a wink.

"With lots of gold fringe!" Claire agreed. "And tassels. I'm thinking tassels everywhere would be quite fun."

It was hard to keep a straight face when Ares was looking at the two of us in such abject horror.

"You know what it really needs?" I said in a conspiratorial whisper. "A cat! Vendetta would just love to—"

Ares grasped my hand. "We must go now," he said, the almost panicked tone of his voice sounding utterly ridiculous on a god of war.

"I love you, Claire," I said.

"I love you, too," she promised.

And then Ares flashed me back to my bedroom before I could cause any more mischief.

"You are a menace," he said, and disappeared.

CHAPTER 53

The house didn't seem the same without Claire in it.
Even Evangeline was not her usual acerbic self. She did
pop in when Michael and I were meeting with Pandora,
Ulysses, and Lizzie about the plans for the new village
and the schoolhouse.

"You need to find an unmarried young schoolmaster," the ghost informed me. "Perhaps some handsome Scottish lad like your husband."

"What?" I asked, confused. "Why should that be a
criterion?"

This abrupt outburst drew questioning looks from
everyone until Pandora said, "Miss Evangeline. I can
feel her in the air."

"For Lizzie," Evangeline replied. "She's a widow
now. You can't expect her to spend her whole life stuck
out here on this island with no male companionship,
can you?"

I looked speculatively at Lizzie, with her honey blonde hair and her soft brown eyes. Good Lord, I'd wager she wasn't even thirty yet. Evangeline certainly had a point.

"I'll see what I can do," I promised her.

When our business was concluded, Pandora and her husband went off to their cabin and Lizzie took the children away to her cottage. Michael and I sat on the porch for several hours, enjoying the night, and feeling a bit abandoned with the house so empty and quiet. A heavy fog had rolled in, blanketing the house in white and making it seem even more isolated and lonely.

"What am I going to tell Raina?" I asked him. "I promised her I'd bring her daughter home. It was bad enough when I thought I was going to have to tell her that Claire wanted to stay in Georgia, but how am I ever going to explain *this*?"

Michael was silent for a moment and then he said, "Tell her that she got her wish. Raina said she wanted Claire to find a man who loved her and would take care of her, a man who was strong enough to share her life."

"I suppose she did," I replied. "It makes you think that you should be careful what you wish for, doesn't it?"

"It does," Michael said distractedly. "Cin, your magic isn't running amuck again, is it?"

"Of course not," I assured him. "Why?"

He pointed toward the road to the village. "Does that look like another ghostly army to you?"

There were lights glowing in the mist and the muffled sound of people moving through the night. The fog was so thick that it wasn't until they'd almost reached the house that I realized it was Pandora, carrying a lantern with Ulysses at her side, and what looked like the entire village following along behind her. Michael and I stood and walked to the edge of the porch.

"What's going on?" I asked her.

"Your ship's comin' tonight," she replied.

"How do you know that?" Michael asked.

"I know same way I knew you was comin'," she said, as if that answered his question.

"There's a full moon tonight," I pointed out. "No ship would try to run through the blockade at the full moon."

I glanced at Michael skeptically. Pandora saw it and leveled a scolding look at me which I'd only seen her use on Ginny and the other children. "The Guédé are death spirits," she informed us. "They told me when you was comin' and they talkin' to me again tonight. Best go pack your things."

Michael and I followed her into the house. There wasn't much to pack. Michael and I lived our lives out of trunks and we'd grown accustomed to not making ourselves too comfortable in one place. Looking around the big bedroom, though, I wished for a moment that we could have made this place the exception. Two weeks ago I would never have thought I would become so attached to this island.

Evangeline materialized in front of me while I was folding the last of my clothes into the trunk.

"You're leaving," she said flatly.

"You knew I would, eventually."

She looked so wounded that I felt guilty for going. I couldn't imagine what it would be like to be in the world and not be able to communicate with anyone around you.

"Evangeline," I said softly. "You've had your revenge now. Adrien Boucher is dead and there's nothing more for you to do here. Why don't you move on to where you're supposed to—"

With one last look of contempt she was gone. I knew she was still in the house. She was just angry with me. I hoped that eventually she would come to see that I had to go. There were evil things in this world that needed my attention.

"Don't you worry none about her," Pandora said. "I'll talk to her and I'm sure Miss Lizzie will too. She sure loved this plantation, Miss Evangeline did."

"She still does," I said. "I'm sure that would mean a lot to her if you acknowledged her presence. And take care of that horrible cat of hers. For whatever reason, she really does love that beast."

Ulysses brought some men up and they carried our trunks down to the waiting wagon. As we left the yard I looked back at the house. Evangeline was standing on the second story's wide balcony in her bottle green evening gown. She raised one hand to me in farewell and I waved back. Then she marched back into the house through the open porch doors, Vendetta scampering after her.

I walked with the people, *my people*, down the oak-lined drive to the dock. Michael and I said our good-byes to Hector, Cassandra, and Perseus. I felt a tugging at my coat and turned to see Ginny McCready walking behind me.

"Are you ever comin' back?" she asked.

"Maybe not for a while, but I promise I'll be back before you're an old married lady," I told her.

She scrunched her nose up. "I told you, I ain't never gettin' married!"

I chuckled and was about to reply when Lizzie rushed up, the baby asleep in her arms. "I was worried I'd miss you," she said.

I hugged her swiftly, ran my fingers over the infant's curly red hair, and we walked together to the dock.

"What if I can't do this?" she asked.

I laughed. "Lizzie, I don't know anyone more capable than you of running this plantation. Not many women would face down a mob with a rifle, you know. You were like a mama bear protecting her cubs. It was really quite a sight."

"Well, it helped that I had vampires at my back," she said.

"You'll do fine," I assured her. "Besides, I don't think you'll have any more trouble."

Lizzie laughed. "What I wouldn't give to hear what they're saying about us in Savannah right now! I can guarantee you it's going to be a long time before anyone from the mainland gets brave enough to come out here again."

"That was the plan," I said. "Vampires are forbidden from meddling in human affairs. I think it's only proper that humans not meddle in mine."

Pandora was standing on the dock, looking much as she had when I'd first seen her. I looked out over the still inlet, wondering if she'd been wrong about the ship. Then I heard it, the soft sloshing sound of oars moving through the water. I smiled when I saw the rowboat come out of the fog. I could make out Devlin's tall, broad form and another man at the oars. Justine was at the bow, her silver-blonde hair shining against her dark cloak. They pulled up to the dock and Justine stood, looking like Venus rising from the sea, and leaped out of the boat. She wrapped her arms around me and I held her close.

"I have missed you so much, *mon amie*," she said. Obviously our little spat was over.

"Oh, I missed you too, Justine," I replied, not realizing until this moment how much that was true. It had only been two weeks, but it seemed like a year since I had seen them last.

She smoothed my hair back. "You look well."

I smiled. "I am well."

The next moment Devlin was there and I was swallowed in his massive embrace, the top of my head only reaching the center of his chest.

"Hello, little one," he said.

I smiled up at him. "How did you know we'd be here, instead of in Savannah?"

"We didn't," Devlin replied. "But Savannah's harbor is now impassable. We thought we'd come ashore here and go overland to the city."

"Have you got your sea legs yet?" I asked.

He scowled. "Let's not bring that up," he said. "Nor the means of transportation Justine has arranged for our journey home."

I knew Justine well enough to know that she would never travel on any ship that wasn't Blood Cross, so I didn't understand Devlin's sour expression. I turned back to her.

"What is he talking about?"

"The ship from hell is what I'm talking about," Devlin groused.

"It was the only one in port and I didn't want to wait any longer," Justine said defensively. "Besides, not many vessels would travel these waters right now."

Devlin snorted and turned his attention to Lizzie. "So, is this young lady the cause of all our troubles?" he asked good-naturedly.

"No," I replied. "This is Lizzie. Claire won't be returning with us."

"Did something happen?" Justine asked worriedly. "*Merde*, I knew I should have come with you."

"Nothing like that," I said. "It's rather a long story."

Ginny piped up, "Miss Claire married Ares and now she lives on Olympus Mountain."

"All right, maybe it's not such a long story," I admitted. "But the details are very convoluted. I'll tell you everything when we get to the ship."

Since the row boat wouldn't hold our trunks, the men loaded them into the island's boat so that Ulysses could take us out to the ship. While they were doing that I left Justine talking to Lizzie and I went to speak to Pandora.

"Come with me," I said. "You and Ulysses, come with me tonight."

"Why would I be wantin' to do that?" she asked, surprised.

"I owe you a great debt for teaching me how to tame the black magic, Pandora. I have a ship waiting. I'll take you both up north to a free state. Or to England, France . . . wherever you want to go. I could take you to Liberia," I offered, thinking of the country that was founded by free slaves from America.

Pandora snorted. "Why would I want to go to Liberia? I ain't no African."

"You set me free. Let me do the same for you."

"I am free, Miss Cin. Adrien Boucher was more of a slave than I am. A man who don't know his true self is a man who's chained. I don't need no white man's piece of paper to tell me who I am. I'm a New Orleans voodoo queen. You keep your promises about how this plantation's gonna be run and we'll consider both of our debts paid."

"I can do that, my friend," I replied.

"Cin," Michael called. "We need to go now."

I boarded the boat with Michael, Devlin, Justine, and the sailor from the Blood Cross ship. As Ulysses pulled away from the dock, Michael and I turned to wave goodbye. I felt a lump catch in my throat as the people of Devil's Island were swallowed by the fog, disappearing into one more chapter of my very long life.

"Is that a tear, *mo ghraidh*?" Michael asked, brushing his fingers across my cheek.

"Maybe just a little one," I replied.

It's strange how some people sneak into your heart so unexpectedly. I'd lost Fiona, Archie, almost everything connecting me to the human world, and then I'd come here. Perhaps this was what Morrigan had had in mind all along. Maybe it wasn't about saving Claire, or thwarting Boucher, maybe it was about binding me to humanity once again. Or maybe it was about freeing my soul, making me embrace the darkness as well as the light within me. I would probably never understand Morrigan's motives but, for once, I was glad of them.

The sailor, a man named Harrison, directed Ulysses through the murky fog. The longer we travelled, the more

I began to wonder what sort of ship Justine had found. The steamer that had brought us to America had a draft of perhaps ten feet. We were going far enough out to sea to accommodate twice that depth. I was about to voice this observation when the fog parted and she was suddenly before us, causing my breath to catch in my throat.

No wonder Devlin had called her the ship from hell.

CHAPTER 54

She looked like the pirate ship that haunted every sailor's nightmares. She was a behemoth of a ship, a four-masted galleon with sixty guns marching along her decks. Great black sails rose up into the night sky, the red Templar cross emblazoned on the bonaventure mizzen. By the gods, she was gorgeous. The steamers were faster and the ironclads were tougher, but nothing compared to the beauty of a galleon. She wouldn't outrun any of the Union gunboats, but I doubted that any of them would give chase to something with sixty cannons that looked like the devil's own ship.

"Devlin, now I understand your derogatory comments," I said. "She's big, but she's not a smooth sail. You must be miserable."

He glanced at Justine. "That's not why I call it the ship from hell," he replied grimly. "When you figure it out, though, just remember it wasn't my idea. This is all Justine's fault."

Justine started mumbling in a torrent of French and I looked worriedly at Michael. He shrugged and we both turned, looking up expectantly as we came alongside the ship. The name on the side of it explained everything. It read: *The Belladonna's Revenge.*

I turned to Justine. "Please tell me this isn't what I think it is," I said.

She looked at me sheepishly and shrugged. The sailors threw down the rope ladder and Michael gestured for me to go first, though I thought it had less to do with gallantry and more to do with his wish to admire the view from below. I swung onto the deck, looking around in dread. Sure enough, there was Belladonna standing on the stern deck, looking as perfectly beautiful as ever. Her curly, jet black hair was down around her shoulders and her lavender eyes sparkled in her flawless, heart-shaped face. She was wearing a dark blue buccaneer's coat with falls of white lace at her throat and wrists, breeches, tall black boots, and a cutlass strapped at her tiny waist.

"Cin!" she called out happily. "Welcome aboard!"

Michael came up behind me and cursed softly under his breath. I glanced back at him, thinking of the last time we'd all been together. He must have been remembering the same thing because he slipped his hand around my waist and pulled me close in a proprietary gesture.

Cautiously we walked to the stern. "Bel, you're supposed to be on Rose Island," I reminded her.

She smiled. "Yes, I'm sure that's what Sinclair is thinking right now too. I have to tell you, Cin, that while my brief visit to Edinburgh didn't turn out exactly as I'd planned, it did put the spark back into my marriage. He may not love me like he once did, but he won't give me up either. Now I run, and he chases. The fun part, of course, is when he catches me."

That was slightly more than I wanted to know.

"You do realize we're headed to Scotland?" Michael asked. "And the King of the Western Lands has promised to take your head if you ever set foot on those shores again."

"Oh, we won't get that far," she scoffed. "Sinclair is only three days behind me and he has a much faster ship."

I shook my head, wondering how I'd once again gotten in the middle of Bel and Sinclair's marital squabbles. I hoped that this time she would have her own husband on her mind enough that she'd keep her eyes off of mine. I wasn't sure if Justine still harbored any resentment over what had happened in London with Archie, but if she did this certainly made us even.

"Oh, cheer up, you two!" Bel said. "It'll be fun. It's been *centuries* since I've run a blockade."

I sighed and leaned against Michael. "Just in case she gets us killed, have I told you yet today how much I love you?" I asked.

Michael chuckled. "Don't worry. I doubt Poseidon himself could kill that woman. But just in case this is our last night on earth, how would you like to spend it, *mo ghraidh*?"

I wrapped my arms around his waist and looked up into his blue eyes. "I think I'd like to split my last bottle of whisky with Devlin and Justine, and then retire to our cabin."

He growled and kissed me. "Have I told you yet today how much I love you, Cin Craven?"

"Not yet," I replied. "But if you'll take me to bed you can show me."

EPILOGUE

Mount Olympus

Her angry footsteps echoed through Ares's temple, contrasting sharply with the soft whisper of the raven-feather cloak against the marble floor. She marched into the room, defiantly coming to a stop in front of the war god, languidly sprawled across his marble throne.

"Morrigan," he said, unimpressed. "To what do I owe the displeasure of your company?"

"I want her back," the goddess demanded.

"Who?" Ares asked dispassionately.

"Claire Macgregor Mahone," Morrigan replied.

That got his attention. Ares sat up on his throne and leaned forward, his fingers flexing against the marble.

"That will never happen," he said coldly.

"She's a Celt. She's my subject and I want her back."

"She's *my* wife," Ares roared. "And you'll not be

getting her back. I don't care if she was once your subject, she's here now and here she will stay. Besides, who are you to quibble over territory? Your vampires run all over mine and you don't see me complaining about it."

Morrigan cocked one black brow at him. "From what I understand you haven't been in a position to complain about anything for quite some time."

Ares stood menacingly. "Go back to Tir na n'Óg, Phantom Queen, before I—"

Morrigan held her hand out and a sword flashed into her palm. "I will fight you for her."

Ares leapt down from the dais, smiling, and drew his own sword. "You cannot win," he said.

"Neither can you," Morrigan replied. "So it appears we are at an impasse."

"What is the meaning of this?" Claire demanded, drawing their attention as she entered the hall. Then her eyes lit on Morrigan. "It's you! You're the one who gave me the urn. How is it you're here?"

Ares jerked his head around in surprise. "You gave her the urn? Why would you do such a thing, Morrigan?"

Morrigan rolled her eyes. "Well, I certainly wouldn't have done it if I'd known this would happen, now would I?"

"What is she talking about?" Claire whispered to her husband.

"She wants me to return you to her," Ares replied. "And I have refused."

"Well, I should hope so!" Claire said indignantly. "I'm the mother of your child."

"And therein lies the problem," Morrigan said. "You've taken one of my people and now you're adding offspring to your pantheon. I demand remuneration. It is my right."

Ares narrowed his eyes, irritated that the goddess was correct. "What do you want?" he asked.

"If you won't give me the girl, then I'll take the first female child of your union as compensation."

"The hell you will!" Claire fumed, her hands flying to her belly. "You are not getting my baby!"

"This one is a boy," Morrigan stated. "I have no use for him."

Claire felt a surge of happiness at the news she was carrying a boy. Ares would like that. Then she became slightly offended on her child's behalf.

"What do you mean you have no use for him?" she asked. "What use would you have for my daughter?"

Morrigan took a step toward Claire and found the tip of Ares' sword resting just below her chin.

"Put away your weapon, war god. I will not harm her," Morrigan scoffed and batted the sword away. She continued forward, unchallenged, until she was standing directly in front of Claire.

As Morrigan raised her hands, Claire's eyes widened in apprehension at the sight of the goddess's long, shiny black fingernails, sharp as a raven's talons. But

Morrigan was true to her word and all she did was gently rest her palms against Claire's temples.

Abruptly, visions flashed through Claire's head, images of a girl, and Claire knew instinctively that this young woman was her daughter. She saw her face, and her destiny. Then the images shifted and changed. Morrigan showed Claire the past and the future, laid it bare before her, and suddenly Claire understood . . . everything.

When Morrigan took her hands away, Claire staggered backward. Ares wrapped one arm around her waist and pulled her protectively to his side.

"Does Cin know?" Claire asked the goddess.

Morrigan shook her head. "No, and you mustn't tell her. She isn't ready to know what the future brings."

"Claire, I don't know how much you can trust anything she shows you," Ares warned. "It could all be a trick."

Claire shook her head. "No, she shows me the truth."

"How do you know?" he asked.

"I just do," she replied. "If I refuse to give her up, what will happen?"

Once again Morrigan laid her hands on Claire. It only took a few seconds before Claire pulled away, shaking her head as if that could somehow dispel what she'd seen.

"All right," Claire said softly. "I agree."

"*Kardia mou*, you do not have to do this," Ares protested. He narrowed his eyes at Morrigan. "You never wanted Claire. This was what you were after all along. What sort of scheme are you brewing, Phantom Queen?"

Morrigan's face took on a hard edge. "The deal is done," she said with finality. "I will return when the child is born."

The goddess turned on her heel and strode out of Ares' temple. Once she cleared the doors, a satisfied smile spread across her face.

I love it when a plan works perfectly, she thought.